I Cry For Innocence

by

Theresia M. Quigley

Canadian Cataloguing in Publication Data

Quigley, Theresia - 1940

I Cry For Innocence

ISBN - 1-894372-16-6
      1. World War, 1939-1945 – Japan -- Fiction. 2. World War, 1939-1945 – Personal narratives, German -- Fiction. I. Title.
      PS8583.U343I2 2002   C813'.54   C2002-902899-X
      PR9199.3.Q53I2 2002

Typesetter: Sonya Sullivan

Cover Design: Dawn Drew, INK Graphic Design Services Corp.

Printed and bound in Canada

DREAMCATCHER PUBLISHING INC.
1 Market Square
Suite 306 Dockside
Saint John, New Brunswick, Canada E2L 4Z6
www.dreamcatcher.nb.ca

COMMENTS ABOUT THE NOVEL

I Cry for Innocence is a fascinating and moving story of civilians – particularly of one courageous woman and her three small children – caught , through no fault of their own, in the far-reaching tentacles of the second world war. At first, we see Liesel, her husband Willi and their three little girls, a two-year-old and six-week-old twins, living happily in the Dutch East Indies, unaware that they are about to be victimized by a conflict spawned in a Europe which they have left many years earlier.

Soon after war breaks out, Willi, a kind and peace-loving man, is arrested and interned by the Dutch simply because he is German. Overwhelmed by accounts of the German invasion of Holland, former friends become enemies overnight and do not raise a finger to help Liesel and her babies, despite the fact that she is half Dutch. She and the children are placed under detention and are eventually sent to Japan.

Liesel's struggle to sustain herself and her youngsters amidst mostly hostile circumstances is riveting. It is a story of love and loyalty which endures despite seemingly insuperable odds. Although *I Cry for Innocence* is not at all preachy, it shows clearly how in wartime it is the innocent who suffer most. This is a story in which every line rings true.

Allison Mitcham
Professor emeritus
Université de Moncton

I Cry for Innocence does more than tell an interesting story, for in a strange but very real way, Theresia Quigley succeeds in having Liesel's odyssey connect us to the Human Heart that binds us all: to that place deep within where heroes as well as villains can emerge in each of us especially during times of suffering and stress, and where we all play out our destinies. We have in this biographical account an amazing tale of adventure and survival, and yet, in the final analysis, because it is the story of a German who did not "know" and who "was not there," we have also, and most poignantly, a rare account of decency and of trust betrayed, of the shame and of the soul-rending guilt which tears apart the hearts of all of us who are of German roots and "cry for innocence."

Barbara Fiand
Cincinnati, Ohio

I found *I Cry for Innocence* an absolutely engrossing read and, as each "adventure" unfolded, I was completely caught up in Liesel and the children's lives. The book expresses so well the reality of war from a civilian's perspective. There have been quite a few stories in the media lately concerning the "guilt" of Germans, as well as the whole concept of guilt/innocence in any war-like situation. I think that *I Cry for Innocence* is very timely indeed from that perspective.

Dawn Arnold
President
Northop Frye International Literary Festival

To My Sisters

ACKNOWLEDGEMENTS

My sincere thanks to Dr. Allison Mitcham, who first suggested that I put pen to paper; to my husband, Louis, and to my children, for their help and love over the years; and to my sisters, my partners in this adventure. Many thanks also to my colleagues at the Department of English, Université de Moncton, for their support, and to the University for the sabbatical leave to help me finish this book, as well as to my many friends for advice and encouragement.

Author's Note

This book has been a long time in the making. In fact, I may have been writing it my entire life. In writing it, I have, of course, used my imagination. But much of it is also based on memory and on my mother's journal and the stories she told me about our life in Indonesia and Japan during the trauma of World War II. And so, it is a multi-layered creation, the weaving together of biography, memory and imagination written in prose mostly, and in poetic form, when I could not say it otherwise. It is also a work of several voices, because I felt that one voice could not have told the whole story.

Most of the characters in the novel are based on actual people with different names, but they are, of course, also creations of the mind. Liesel Fiand, my mother, is portrayed as she was, but she is also part of me, and part of what I think she was, and certainly, part of what she will always be in my heart and in my memory.

I wrote this book as a kind of necessity: because it is a good story; because it is my story; because it is a story many friends told me must be told, but, mostly, because it is a testimony to the strength and the love of one woman, a German woman, an ordinary woman, who rose above the ordinary and made a difference.

I

Mama was the sixth child of twelve. She was born in 1901 in the industrial heartland of the Ruhrgebiet, *near Essen, Germany. Tiny, pretty and smart, with a mass of auburn curls and dark brown eyes, she was the darling of her father, Mathias Hoegner, a foreman at the giant steel mill in Oberhausen.*

The family's front door, one of many of a row of gray brick houses each connected with the next through shared walls and common cellars, was only a stone's throw away from the huge iron gates of the mill, and she would often run there in the evening to meet her father and help him carry his lunch pail home. -And what have you done today, littlest one?- he would ask her, taking her small hand in his, and she would share with him her daily adventures.

It was he who encouraged her to sing, recognizing early on that she had a remarkably clear soprano voice with perfect pitch. They sang together in the local church choir and performed at charity events. Opa Hoegner *also helped her overcome her early stage fright, telling her to think of the heads she faced in the darkened auditorium as so many heads of cabbage in a field and of herself as the lark singing to them in the early morning.*

1

It was her voice also that first attracted Papa when he heard her sing at a charity affair in sun-drenged Surabaya, Java, half-way across the world from her gray home town. A dark-haired slip of a girl in a white dress, singing Schubert's "Heidenroeslein." He thought he had never heard anything so beautiful.

Papa was a wealthy businessman by then – well established in Surabaya's Dutch/German community, and regarded by the matrons 'in-the-know' as the catch of the season. Mama had come to Java as a governess/companion to the Jensens, a well-to-do Dutch family. He managed to be introduced, and proposed marriage within weeks, and she promptly refused. He was only twenty-eight and she was thirty-six. She saw herself ageing, while he was still in his prime. But he would hear none of her objections and, of course, in the end, he prevailed. Tenderness and charm were part of his southern German heritage; optimism and perseverance had made him a success, and those were forces she could not fight forever.

- I will be old when you are still a young man, Willi.

- You will never be old to me!

- I've been alone too long.

- Time to be alone no longer.

- I've learned to be by myself. I like my independence.

- But, Liesele, you want children! You are made for love!

Hannele was born eight months after they were married, and twenty months later, identical twin girls, Baerbel and Resel, made their appearance, only weeks before the storm broke over the Dutch East Indies, and Asia was caught in the grip of war.

*****

The afternoon is hot and sultry. Sarangan is caught in a heat wave usually reserved for Surabaya this time of the year. People come to the lake, the mountains, the refreshing breezes to get away from the unbearable humidity of the city. But the heat of the city has crept up to the mountains, just like all the other troubles. One can't get away from it. The thing has tentacles that reach everywhere!

Liesel rearranges the pillows under the mosquito netting, turning them over, yet again, to the cooler side. She must get some rest.

-What will happen next? - she wonders. - It certainly has been a dreadful morning! But at least all is quiet for now, and the children are finally napping. God knows how all this will end… -

It had started with the nursemaid packing all her belongings early in the morning without saying a word. She would not respond to any of Hannele's babble and simply shrugged when Liesel asked her what she was doing. At the door she stopped, her brown eyes avoiding Liesel's. "Father sick," she mumbled under her breath and ran down the steps towards the lake.

Looking out of her window, Liesel had watched a mass exodus of the mostly native hotel staff carrying bundles of all shapes and sizes. Some were running, some walking, looking about furtively. *Oma* Becker, still in her housecoat, her gray hair not yet braided into the usual tight crown around her head, was standing on the

3

front steps of the hotel, arguing in a loud voice, bordering on hysteria, with the chief gardener, a large, burly fellow, who smiled too much and perspired profusely. He was in the process of leaving with the others, his belongings, and some that were obviously not his, loaded onto the hotel's large green wheelbarrow. *Oma* Becker was making a feeble attempt to rescue some of the items before he had a chance to move away, and Liesel watched in disbelief as the fellow simply pushed his former employer out of the way with a large hairy arm and, smirking disdainfully, followed the others.

- The place is practically empty now,- she thinks. - But who can blame them? They are not stupid. They know that something is wrong and don't want to get caught in the middle. Working for a German hotel is not politically smart right now. So it's best to go into hiding somewhere for the time being and let the white people fight it out.... We're at war! Germany and Holland, at war, and former friends don't speak to one another any more.... And so, smarter people than I stay at home with their husbands and don't go traipsing into the mountains to get away from the heat, whatever that heat may be.... -

Liesel closes her eyes and tries in vain to relax and to pretend that this is all a bad dream.

...-I am not alone here in this godforsaken hotel with one old hysterical lady hotel manager and three small children. And Willi ..., oh why did I listen to him! Maybe if I had been there with him, they would at least have taken us away together. I would not have minded that, as long as we were together. God! What a difference that would make, to be with him, to know that he is safe, at least for now. It's the uncertainty, the not knowing what

they are doing to him, the powerlessness of not knowing anything!
-

But the twins had been so very sick! Covered with a heat rash from head to toe, and nothing seemed to help. Resel had cried all night and had kept Baerbel awake. Liesel had not had a good night's sleep for over a week, and the heat seemed to be getting worse. When Willi had found her in tears in the nursery, nothing would do but to pack them into the car and head for the mountains. They could stay there in the comfort of the Becker Hotel, and he would come to pick them up in a couple of weeks when the twins were feeling better and the heat in Surabaya had somewhat abated.

-You need your rest. I should have seen this long ago. This place is not healthy for you or the children. And stop worrying! Nothing is going to happen to me!-

But while he was happily chatting and arranging things, Liesel kept thinking of the three Dutch military policemen who had burst into their bedroom a few weeks earlier in the middle of the night, searching all the drawers, - her private things -, while she was sitting with the sheets draped around her, staring in disbelief. They had taken Willi in handcuffs to be interrogated.

In the middle of the night! … The pounding at the door … the bright lights … and three strangers staring at them through the mosquito netting. -Get up *mijnheer* ! You will have to come with us!- He had tried to protest, but they had simply repeated their demand while they searched through her lingerie. Three horrible days of questioning had produced nothing. In the end, they had had to let him go.

-Look, Liesel, that was four weeks ago.- Willi had argued. -They would have come back for me by now, if they'd dared. I am a private citizen! What could they possibly want with me, anyway?- He believed that the war would be over in a matter of weeks, and then everything would go back to normal. -They know that all this foolishness has to stop. Europe can't afford this kind of thing again. And when it's all over, we'll all have to be friends again, won't we? -

Ever the optimist, he did not believe the stories that their friends had brought back from Germany. Bert and Greta Klausner had returned from leave in Hamburg and had told stories of looting and violence, Jewish slogans, stores deliberately ransacked, and the slightest resistance met with force.

- Bert likes to hear himself talk.- Willi had scoffed. -He heard all this second and third hand. People always exaggerate. Who would deliberately throw good merchandise into the Elbe? The German police would not put up with something like that. And beating up old people in the streets? Come on! In Germany? Some *Dummkoepfe* might not care for the Jews, but can you believe for one moment the German people would allow something like this to go on? -

It went against his very nature to accept the possibility of man's inhumanity. He was basically an innocent, and that is why she loved him.

- But what if it is true… ? Could it not be true, some of it, anyway?- She knows that rumors do not start from nothing. - What will they do to him and to the other German men on the islands? What will they do to all of us? Innocence is no protection in war time, and hate, revenge for the wrongs of others are accepted, even expected, in war…. We would have had nearly two more weeks together, if I'd stayed where I belong. God! To be able to go back in time and not be burdened with what I know now. We were so happy! …I would enjoy every tiny moment. I would savour it. I would store it in my memory to help me through the today, through the now. -

It was his hands that she had fallen in love with. He thought it funny when she told him this. But it was true. There was something so reassuring about them. They were dependable hands. Large and strong and warm. And his eyes, gray eyes that smiled and would surprise her, flashing suddenly, making her feel weak inside. - I can feel it now, that strange, warm sen-sation…. Oh God, let him be safe! Make them give him back to me! -

***

When she had not heard from him for a few days, she tried to call Surabaya. But the operator had said that the lines were busy. Later she said that the phone was out of order and, finally, that it had been disconnected. Liesel left the children with *Oma* Becker and drove down to Surabaya. Something was terribly wrong; she had to find out what had happened.

The house was padlocked. Rough wooden planks criss-crossed the windows. A big sign read that trespassers would be jailed. -

She was no trespasser! This was her house, her home, … or was it? -

She tried to look into the dining room from the glass doors at the back veranda. The place was bare. Not a stick of furniture. The walls naked. The spot where Hannele's portrait had been was a light patch on the wall. -Who would take that picture? A little curly-haired girl with a sweet smile. Their little girl. Who would take a picture of their little girl? It was cruel! And where was Willi? How could this happen in so short a time? -

There was not a soul to be seen anywhere. Back on the street, Liesel caught sight of the house-boy, but he stared and ran. At Lotte's, the servant looked flustered and said that *Mevrouw* was not in. Lotte's husband worked for the Dutch government and Liesel had known them even before she had met Willi. Their car was in the driveway. That meant her friend was somewhere in the house. A gentle push, and the servant let go of the door. And Lotte was there, looking worried and embarrassed.

-Walter won't like your being here. I'm not supposed to talk to you,- she said.

-What is the matter with you? We are friends!-

-You made your choice when you married a German.- She spat out that last word, like an oath. - Walter says it does not matter that you are half Dutch. You're German now! And you're not supposed to be here!-

-Where is Willi? What has happened? I've been in Sarangan with the children and no one called me! You did not even think to call me! -

Lotte would not meet her eyes. - They took him to the detention centre earlier this week.- Her voice was flat, no feeling. What had happened to the love they had shared? -And the day before yesterday, they sold all the contents of your house, first come, first serve. Curtains, right off the windows. Margo VanJan got your entire Rosental dinner service for *ten* gulden. – Lotte actually sounded envious.

Liesel left her standing at the door without another word. At the detention centre, she was told bluntly that her husband was not there. Precious time was lost begging for more information but to no avail. They were all busy, and she was wasting their time, and would she please leave. But outside, on the stairwell, one of the clerks waited for her and whispered hurriedly that the German men had left that very noon for internment near Batavia. -They are stopping along the way to pick up more men, and the buses are old, - he added significantly, and signalled with his head in the direction of the main auto route.

The road was dusty and badly paved. Twisting and turning around fields parched by the lack of rain. Behind every curve Liesel thought she could catch a glimpse of a bus. The heat was oppressive and her head was pounding. And then, finally, there they were! Men milling around the side of the road. Guards shouting orders, cursing. Utter confusion. She screeched to a halt and ran along the side of the bus.

-Willi! Willi!-

-He's on the one just ahead of us! - someone shouted.

Back into the car and on at breakneck speed. Nothing mattered now. He was just ahead. A mile, maybe half a mile. And yes, there was the other bus, parked at a filling station with men in the process of boarding. She ran along the windows, jumping up to see, screaming his name, waving frantically.

-Willi! Willi Fiand! Your wife is here! -

- Let the man out, will you !-

And he was holding her to him, and she was crying. Stupid tears! All along the way, she had promised herself that, no matter what happened, she would not break down and cry. When she saw him – no tears! But the minute she was in his arms, her eyes betrayed her!

-It won't be long, - he said. -A few weeks, that's all. Don't worry about me, and don't fret about the house. I'll buy you a nicer one! -

One of the guards pushed him roughly to get back on the bus. Another one told him to let them be.

- Hold me, hold me, just for a moment longer! -

And then he was gone, and she was running along with the bus until it picked up speed and was lost in the dust. When she got back to Sarangan, *Oma* Becker said that she looked different. In the mirror, she saw that her hair was streaked with gray....

***

It is so very quiet outside. Almost too quiet. Hannele comes into the room, rubbing her eyes. The twins are still sleeping, though it is close to their feeding time. Then, suddenly, a screech of tires! A car door is slammed! Running feet and someone shouting! Liesel's heart begins to pound. This has happened before... a few weeks ago in Surabaya. She gets up quickly and puts on a housecoat. They won't find her unprepared this time.

The door bursts open and two men in uniform stare at her. Liesel knows one of them, a young man with straight blond hair which is always hanging over his eyes. He works at the police depot in the village and regularly checks the pleasure boats on Lake Sarangan to make sure that they meet all the safety regulations. She used to see him most afternoons when she went riding along the lake.

- The hotel is being vacated and everyone is leaving, *Mevrouw* Fiand, - he says. His voice is shaking, and he does not look at her. -You have an hour to pack your things! - His face is quite red, and he turns quickly to leave.

The twins start crying simultaneously.

-I have three children under the age of two, and their *babu* left this morning. I can't possibly be ready at such short notice! -

11

The second policeman now springs into action. He is small and fat, his uniform stained with perspiration. He has been waiting for just such an opportunity to speak. Four steps and he is in the middle of the room.

-Look at this! - he shouts. -Just look at this fancy room, while our friends and families are hiding in the cellars of Holland! They receive no warning, *Mevrouw,* when your dirty countrymen decide to flatten their homes! Consider yourself lucky that you have one full hour! - He turns and marches out grabbing his friend by the arm. At the door he turns again. -One hour, *Mevrouw!* - he barks.

Oma runs in. She looks so old! - What will they do to us? Where will they take us? -

She has been hoping that the officials in Surabaya would be too busy to bother with Sarangan, and that they would forget about her hotel until after the war. Now her world is tumbling around her feet. Liesel already knows what that feels like.

-I have to get the children ready. Can you give me a hand? -

-Give you a hand? What about my things? I'll never make it in time!- She turns and runs around the room, frantically grabbing a pillow, a blanket, and then rushes out.

-I'll throw a few things into a suitcase, and then I'll nurse the twins. Surely they won't move me with a child at my breast!- Liesel realizes, with sudden certainty, that if she is going to survive this, she will have to do it on her own.

12

II

Papa was not a tall man - possibly five foot nine -, with broad shoulders and strong, capable hands. Pictures of him at twenty-eight show an intelligent face with a high forehead and strong *eyebrows, his head square-shaped rather than round and his hairline, even then, markedly receding. His eyes were gray-green and kind; they were smiling eyes, which, while eagerly observant, hinted at the mind of an idealist, a dreamer, who would see only the good in people and did not suspect darkness.*

He was born in 1909 in Haslach, a small village on the outskirts of the beautiful medieval city of Freiburg, im Breisgau, *in the heart of the Black Forest region of Germany. And until the day he died, after travelling around the globe and seeing incredible sights, it was this little corner of the world, Freiburg and its cathedral, the* Muenster, *with its Gothic tower, built of stone and light, and the mountains that surround it like a green garland, which were at the center of his heart and longing.*

He was the oldest of three boys. Oma *Fiand had given birth to three children who had all died in infancy. So, of course, Papa, the first to survive, was especially dear to her.*

-He was my heart's delight,- she told me. -So quiet and smart, and always in the books. He could not get enough of books.- She shook her head. -Your Opa *did not like this,- she said. - He thought that Wilhelm wanted to become too big for his place in life. They were always fighting... .-*

-Your Opa *would not let him go to university, you know. Wilhelm had a scholarship, and the village pastor was going to pay for all his other expenses, but* Opa *said no, and that was the end of it. So your Papa ran away from home. He was only sixteen. I went up to his room one morning and found a letter. He had left in the middle of the night. It broke my heart.-*

I can still see her face, heart-shaped and sweet, and her blue eyes full of remembered pain. -He said he would write me, and that I should not worry about him. But he did not write, not for a long, long time. Young people don't think of the hurt they can cause. He did not mean to hurt me, I know. But I waited and waited for a word from him, and then I thought that something bad must have happened to him. For so long a time I waited, and then I thought that he was surely dead.-

Papa worked in Holland and then in Norway, and finally he signed on as a crewmember of a British merchant ship and traveled around the world several times, picking up languages as he went: English, French, Dutch, Norwegian. On shore-leave in Surabaya, he fell ill with typhoid fever and had to be left behind. When his ship stopped there again several months later, he was fully recovered, had made friends, found employment and saved enough money to buy out his contract.

14

He never saw his father again. By the time he wrote home, Opa *had died of an accidental fall at work, and* Oma *was a widow.*

*****

Liesel has only received one letter from Willi in over a month. It was very short, like the ones all the other women had received. She suspects that the men were told not to exceed 25 words. He wrote that he was well; not to worry. He missed her and the children. Could she send him a picture? She was always in his thoughts and in his heart.

Colonel Van Decker, the Dutch officer who checks on the ladies at Rosenhof every morning, has told her that the men are fine but are no longer permitted to write unless there is an emergency. And so she must rely on what she hears from the colonel and try not to listen to the ever-changing rumors of which there seems to be no end of supply: "The men are still near Batavia." - "No, no, they are no longer there." - "They are being moved to the other end of the island." - "No, they are being shipped to Atjeh on Sumatra next week, because the Dutch think the war will last years, and they want the prisoners to be in a more secure place." - "And yes, there is room at the women's internment camp; and yes, everyone will be moved there shortly."

The thought of the Surabaya internment camp makes her shiver. It is a dusty, dirty place and unbearably hot, with barbed wire fences and no washing facilities, or at least not enough for all those women and children. Rumor has it that most of the children are sick and that all the women are fighting.

Liesel does not want to think about it. She has resigned herself to let things happen as they will. It is all beyond her control. But she knows that they are tremendously lucky to be where they are. The air is clear and crisp at Rosenhof, and a cool mountain breeze keeps the temperature at a comfortable level, day and night. They have been here two months now, but things being as they are, this is probably too good to last.

The move from the hotel had turned out to be a lot less traumatic than she had feared. They had had more than three hours to get their things together at the hotel. No one showed up until after eight in the evening, when an army van stopped at the front steps and a tall young man in uniform, whom she had never seen before, ran up to the door and surveyed the scene in the foyer: two babies in baskets, a little girl sleeping on a sofa, two distraught women, and a pile of luggage.

-Well, it looks as though you are ready to go,- he smiled. - Sorry, if I made you wait. -

What a difference from the two earlier ruffians! He had told them that they, together with about a dozen other German women and children who had been vacationing in the mountains, were being taken to Rosenhof, a villa that had been confiscated for the purpose and was only a few miles from Sarangan, higher up in the mountains. Liesel was familiar with the place. It belonged to a Dutch doctor who had returned to Holland when he had become ill with a kidney disease. Airy and bright, with spacious rooms, wide corridors, and large windows overlooking the Sarangan valley and lake, it had extensive grounds, carefully groomed, and even a tennis court. She could hardly believe their good fortune. They were to be placed under house-arrest, but would be free to enjoy the gardens. The large iron gate at the entrance of a wide gravel path leading to the house would be kept locked, and provisions would be brought to the villa as required.

-You might find it a bit crowded, *Mevrouw*, -   the young officer had said, looking at the sleeping babies and Hannele, who had wakened and was by now hanging onto Liesel's skirt. -You'll have one room only, and you'll be the only one with small children. But it is better than the camp... , I think.- He had dropped them off at Rosenhof and helped bring their things inside. She had not seen him since.

Colonel Van Decker, who used to be a regular visitor at the hotel in Sarangan,   had driven up in his gray jeep the first morning after their arrival at Rosenhof and had almost bumped into Liesel, who was just leaving the house to go for a walk with Hannele. A tall, rotund man in his late forties, he often walked with his head bowed as if concentrating on the ground in front of him and regularly collided with a number of immovable objects on his inspection tours.

-This is most unfortunate, *Mevrouw* Fiand, - he stammered when he recognized Liesel.

 She was not quite certain whether he meant her arrest the day before or the war in general. Taking out his boldly checkered handkerchief, he nervously wiped the perspiration from his shining forehead. The few blond strands of hair left to him, now rapidly turning gray, were carefully parted at the side and combed forward at a slant to give the deceiving appearance of plenty.

-I know all the ladies here and … well, …I am sure we can work fine together, … just fine. Er… I check in every morning, you know, of course, … well, just to make sure all is fine. Regulations, you know, er…. And then, oh, well…, one might have an emergency or other. At any rate, *Mevrouw*, … - he smiled tentatively, obviously ill at ease, -I will be at your service.- He clicked his heels together, German fashion, and made a little formal bow.

-How odd!- Liesel thought, hiding a smile. -This is our jailer! It could be worse.- His embarrassed manner caught her completely by surprise, but before she had a chance to form an adequate reply, Hannele came skipping along, smiling brightly .

-*Onkel* Otto!, *Onkel* Otto!- she cried, running up to him and hugging his legs.

-Come visit me?-

-Hannele, this is Colonel Van Decker. He is a very busy man, I'm sure, and you must not hang on to his trousers!- Liesel tried to free the colonel from Hannele's tight hold.

-Is this your little girl?- he asked surprised. -We know each other quite well from Sarangan. Her *babu* told me that she has twin sisters too!- He was on one knee now, stroking Hannele's tight curls.

-Yes, I have three little ones.- Liesel said quietly. She was not asking for special consideration, but he might as well know how things stood.

He got up with a sigh and looked down at her in a strangely kind way. She did not realize how very vulnerable she looked, standing there in front of him, trying so hard to appear unconcerned and independent. The top of her head did not even reach his shoulder.

-*Mevrouw*, I will do what I can for you. Do me the honor of considering me your friend.- He bowed again and strode heavily up the steps of the main house, while Liesel kept Hannele's moist little hand tightly clasped in hers to stop her from chasing after him, and tried to control the tears that suddenly seemed determined to find an escape down her cheeks.

Over the weeks that followed, he had been true to his word. A friend in need. There were still such people in the world, even now.

***

Rosenhof is a large villa with nine bedrooms and several comfortable sitting rooms. But it seems that when twelve women, good enough friends in normal times, are forced to live together in semi-confinement and uncertainty for months on end, tempers are rubbed raw and nerves cry out. A scapegoat is looked for and invariably found. Liesel did not relish that role.

-Is that little brat ever going to stop her infernal screaming at night? I have never in my life experienced anything so nerve-racking!- Christa Braun, a thin woman with straight black hair and a rather sallow complexion, has no children of her own. She is a staunch believer that the greatest kindness one can perform is not to bring children into this terrible world. Liesel experiences a fervent wish that Christa's own mother had shared her daughter's conviction. She is about to enter the dining room, but Frau Braun's comment has her rooted to a spot just outside the door.

-Well, I'm certainly glad that Hans and I never managed to get around to having children.- Wilma Reis yawns. -He was always nagging me about kids. Building a dynasty and all that foolish stuff. He was anxious to leave his name for posterity, I suppose. Though I really can't think that a bunch of little Hansels would improve the world one little bit. I am sure he is a happy man now that I wouldn't hear of getting pregnant in this climate. He was constantly harping about the Fiands too: 'Look at Willi Fiand!'- she mimics. -'They're hardly married and have three almost at once. That's what I call action!' Some action! She's stuck with them now, isn't she!-

Wilma and Hans had been Willi and Liesel's closest friends in Surabaya, and Liesel has difficulty believing the spiteful words she has just overheard.

- You always told me that Hans was the one who did not want children, - *Oma* Becker says, with some surprise. Wilma is her only daughter, but there is little love lost between the two, and Wilma seldom bothers to answer her mother. She is an attractive blond, tall and slim. Her eyes, a pale blue, seem to regard the world around her with mocking disdain. Of all the women at Rosenhof, she seems to mind the war the least. She looks upon it as a kind of personal challenge and is already complaining that Colonel VanDecker, a bachelor, is 'so completely unattractive' and, therefore, not worth her attention.

Liesel takes advantage of the interchange between *Oma* and Wilma to go in for breakfast. There is a pronounced silence, and then Kaete Zimmermann says kindly: - You look dreadfully tired, Liesel. Is Resel not any better this morning?-Liesel has not known Kaete for very long. She and her husband, Bernt, had not belonged to the so-called Surabaya 'inner circle,' but she has been consistently kind to Liesel since they were thrown together at Rosenhof. Kaete is a large woman in her mid-thirties, with light brown, wavy hair which she wears in a loose bun at the nape of her neck. Her eyes are dark and gentle.

-What that child needs is a good spanking.- Christa Braun states categorically. -I have a sister in Bremen who had every one of her kids spoiled hopelessly. She never got a moment's rest until they were six months old.-

-What happened then?- Kaete asks pointedly. -Did she give them away? -

-No, of course not! Somehow they just stopped their nightly tantrums. She always claimed it was some kind of digestive disorder. But my Klaus said that a spanking probably would have put an end to all this nonsense far more effectively and quickly.-

-Sounds like stomach cramps to me. Babies sometimes have them for months.- Irma Kaufman puts in her two-cents worth. Her twelve-year-old daughter, Annegrete, is the only other child at Rosenhof. Irma is usually too sleepy or too lazy to enter a conversation. But now she turns to Annegrete, who listens open-mouthed to the adult conversation, and pats her on the head. -Our Annegretchen never kept her Mami and Papi awake a single night. She was such a dear little angel.-

Liesel feels nauseated. Her head is aching and her heart is pounding. She would like to strike someone. She thinks fleetingly of the regular internment camp. There are many children there, one more crying wouldn't make much difference. But she quickly dismisses the thought. In any event, Resel is too ill. She has a fever and should see a doctor. When the Colonel comes this morning, she will ask him to take them to Sarangan. Even if the clinic doesn't like treating Germans any more, if he brings her, surely, they can't refuse a sick child!

She gulps down a cup of coffee and takes Hannele outside for a walk down to the gate. She might see him before he gets to the main house and must listen to the endless list of complaints from women who have nothing to do all day but feel sorry for themselves.

There is a little guesthouse at the bottom of the hill. It has one large room and a corner kitchenette, also a tiny bathroom facility, and a second, smaller room at the back. A look through the dusty windows reveals a few tools stacked in one corner and two broken chairs piled one on top of the other near the door. It wouldn't take long to clean this up. Some curtains on the windows, a rug on the floor. It would make a cozy little nest.

Hannele is playing with the white gravel at the side of the walk when Liesel hears the now familiar noise of the jeep backfiring down the road. He sees them and stops, jumps out smiling as Hannele runs up to him and then frowns when he sees Liesel's face.

-The little one is still sick,- she stammers. He always calls Resel 'the little one' because she seems so much more fragile and tiny than Baerbel. -Colonel, I really don't want to bother you, but I must see a doctor. Resel cries and cries all night and keeps the whole house awake. No one can get any sleep.- And then her voice breaks and she quickly turns away. He looks so concerned and understanding.

-I think it is you who need some sleep,- he says. -I will check on the ladies, and then we will take you and the little one to Sarangan. My doctor there will see her.-

In Sarangan, they say that Resel will have to stay overnight at the clinic. -An infection and a bit of a fever. There may be some dehydration. She is also cutting four teeth at once and her gums are red and swollen. We'd better keep her here and help her along. Give us a call in the morning, *Mevrouw*. It won't be more than a day or two! -

-She is so small! Oh God! How can I leave her here? - Liesel looks at Colonel VanDecker. -I can't bear it! -

He takes her arm and leads her back to the jeep. -She'll be just fine, just... fine.- he says, but he sounds as upset as she does, and suddenly she feels much better.

-What a great pair we make,- she smiles to herself, and on the way home she finds the courage to ask him about the guest house.

-But you will be all alone there!- he protests.

-It's right on the property, within the gates, and they are locked, as you know. The children will be free to play and cry and make as much noise as they want. I can take my meals with the others. It's just for a place to sleep, Colonel.-

By the time they arrive at Rosenhof, she has him convinced that the move is necessary for the sake of the children. In the morning he will help her set things up.

III

When she was twenty-five, Mama became engaged to Franz Kessner. They planned to save enough money to furnish a flat of their own and then get married. Franz worked for a firm in Essen, and Mama was by then an accomplished couturier.

She had studied the art of dressmaking at a school on the Rhine and had quickly established a small business, which she ran from home. In those days, wealthy clients also often asked her to come to their homes to live and work there until all their particular fashion needs were met. Sometimes this could take weeks and even months. She had met Franz at the home of a family with whom she was staying. The two had become instant friends.

He was a tall, thin man with a shock of yellow hair and a quiet, introspective manner. They both loved books and walks in the country, and life seemed perfect for several years. And then Franz became ill and was diagnosed with tuberculosis. His family had a history of the disease and several had died.

They were of course terrified when Franz became ill and would not think of visiting him at the sanatorium. -I was his only visitor,- Mama told me, and when I asked her why she had not been scared of the disease, she shook her head and smiled.

- For us, you see, there was love. Strong and sure and warm, there was that certainty, larger than hope, that he would pull through, that he would make it. It kept us going. We clung to that certainty until the very end. We were young, of course, and death was not for us!

-I was his link to the outside world.- she said. -Sunday was the only day I could get there. The sanatorium was quite a trip by train and bus. But I was determined to make it, no matter what. And he would ask me to sing for him, the old Lieder that he loved. And the nurses and other patients would come to listen… . I sang for him the day he died. He just lay there, his hand in mine. An when the nurse touched my arm, I knew that he was gone.-

Mama left the sanatorium and went home to pack her bags. -There was nothing left for me there,- she said. -My Papa had died a few years earlier. I had to get away.-

She went to Amsterdam to stay with her mother's family, the Otterloos. They helped her make friends, perfect her Dutch and establish a little business. And then one of her clients offered her the opportunity of a lifetime, - a trip around the world. The Jensens were leaving for Java, and she was invited to come with them. It was too good to miss.

*****

Now that Resel is better, the nights are quiet in the cozy little guesthouse, which Liesel has named *Drei Maedel Haus*. But sleep won't come. Night time is the only time she has to think, and thought is the enemy of slumber.

...-Are you still alive? Now, at this very moment, with the night sky full of friendly stars that shine in my window, do you see the stars? Are you thinking of me?- She tries to concentrate on Willi's face, his dear face, his eyes, his mouth.... But oh, it hurts, and the gnawing ache in her body grows unbearable. So many empty nights of longing and worrying....

No one seems to know where or how the men are. One rumor has it that several have been placed in a special barrack reserved for retributive justice the next time there is a major offensive against Holland. That's what they call it, 'retributive justice.'

She remembers the young Dutch lieutenant, one of several officials who had come to inspect the premises and make their power felt.... -Your husband is one of the ones we have selected for retribution,- he tells her, smiling. He has large white teeth and cold eyes. -There are always a few troublemakers in every group. But we know how to take care of them.- She feels faint and, suddenly, very cold.

-Do you think that this kind of action will stop the bombing?- Her voice trembles. -A few German civilians in a Dutch internment camp halfway across the world. A few men selected for slaughter to revenge slaughter! Do you really think that this will stop the war?- She stares at him.

He shrugs, still smiling, a thin, cold smile. -We must strike back somehow. Some kind of retaliation is necessary. You should thank us on your knees that it isn't you or your children we're taking away for retaliation.- As he speaks, he makes a point of studying the twins who are sitting on their big red play rug. He actually goes over and, bending down, lifts their little faces with his hands. She sees that he has large, ugly hands. Resel starts to cry, and he chuckles and looks back at her, letting his eyes travel slowly up and down, taking in the fear in her eyes.

-He is enjoying this, and he wants me to prolong his enjoyment,- she thinks. And she forces herself to turn away and pick up a book. The letters on the page are swimming before her eyes, and she feels deathly sick. His stare is painful, like an actual touch, demanding a response. She can feel her pulse in her ears and forces herself to breathe slowly, evenly.

And then, quite suddenly, he loses interest. She is not responding as he wishes. The whole thing is beginning to bore him, and he is annoyed that he has started this conversation with her. She feels his anger, cold and dangerous. -You're a strange one,- he says between his teeth. -Why don't you cry? But you're just a crazy German female. You have no feelings and shouldn't be treated like normal women.-

Colonel Van Decker is furious, when she asks him if the stories are true. He turns quite red. -That lousy *Lumpel*! He has no way of knowing if there is such a select group, and who would be in it. It's nothing but rumors. It's something some of them would like to see done, and they make up stories. Don't you worry, *Mevrouw*.-

But Liesel cannot stop worrying. Somehow she knows that Willi is in danger. -I feel it with that cursed certainty that is so strangely part of me. Why can we not touch each other in our thoughts? I know that you are thinking of me. Yes, you are thinking of me! … But if you are dead?… Oh God!… ! With all this anger, does God still care?…-

She gets up. Might as well. No use trying to find rest when the mind will not cooperate. The children are peacefully sleeping. Three even little sighs of happy slumber. She envies them. -To be small again. Too small to worry… to know. -

Outside on the small veranda, which also acts as a front door step to the little house, the night is dark and calm. No lights at the main house. Only the stars in the tropical sky.   -How romantic this could be! But far away, bombs are falling, and not so far away, men are lying behind bars, wondering if they will be alive tomorrow.-

Liesel turns on the light in the little kitchen and makes herself a cup of tea. She gives silent thanks for this little house. Her own little private kingdom. Every morning she cooks breakfast here, but she takes the children to the main house for the big meal of the day. The Colonel stops most mornings for a chat and sometimes has a cup of coffee. Even the ladies are glad to have a place to visit.

She had found an extra table and chairs and other necessary furniture in what used to be the servants' quarters behind the main building. In the large attic of the villa, there were several old rugs, still in good shape, and a number of usable curtains. There was also an old sewing machine, still in working condition, and she is now able to make little outfits for the girls from some of her own cotton dresses and from extra bed linen of which there seems to be an unusually large supply at Rosenhof. The children sleep in the small room at the back, and she has a daybed in the main room, which serves as living/dining/play room during the day. The whole arrangement is cozy and comfortable. She loves her little house.

At first, of course, the idea had not been looked upon with a great deal of enthusiasm. A number of reasons were advanced why Liesel's move was not to be thought of. There was a certain amount of embarrassment, and that did not sit well with most of them. After all, they did not want it to look as though they had driven out a mother and her three small babies. That had really never been their intention. Liesel must not be so easily offended. A comment here or there must not be taken so seriously. In times of crisis people must learn to be more broad-minded and tolerant and less thin-skinned.

But Liesel had simply gone about the business of moving. Weeks ago, when she had kissed Willi good-bye on the dusty road to Batavia, she had faced the fact that she was now basically alone and that decisions concerning her little family were now hers to make and to carry out. Soon the arguments had stopped, but the ladies look at her with a kind of awe that secretly amuses her. She has a calm determination that frightens most of them. But they are glad to have a place to go, to break the boredom of confinement. And children, after all, are quite entertaining in small doses.

The girls are growing so very fast. Hannele, with her brown curls and her large gray eyes, is a sweet-tempered little girl and smart as a whip, and Liesel finds in her, small as she is, a soul-mate of sorts. The child seems to intuit her mother's darker moments and is always there, with a small, warm hand in hers, when she needs it most. Baerbel looks much like Willi. Her eyes are green and her brows are very pronounced. When she frowns, Liesel has to laugh at the resemblance. Resel is smaller. While she looks like her twin, and strangers cannot tell them apart, Liesel is able to detect some of her own features in the child, which have as yet not appeared in Baerbel.

Colonel VanDecker likes to pick up Baerbel in particular, she is less fragile and hugs him tightly. Liesel is glad that he likes children and spends some time with them. They won't grow afraid of a male face or voice. Hannele loves her *Onkel* Otto, and both twins smile and stretch out their arms when he comes to the door. He is a lonely man with no family, and Liesel knows that he has adopted them, in a fashion, as his own.

Of course there are comments about the Colonel's frequent visits to the little guesthouse. -It's so convenient, those cozy chats you have. And no one there to interrupt you.- Wilma does not forget to smile sweetly when says this, and it takes Liesel a moment to understand what is being implied. The ladies all look sheepish. This has obviously been a subject of conversation between them. Only Kaete seems genuinely upset. -Three little girls are plenty of interruption, as you no doubt remember, Wilma, - she points out rather sharply, and that ends the discussion for the moment

-Let them talk. It gives them something to fill their empty lives,- Liesel muses, as she sips her tea outside on the veranda under the night sky. -The Colonel is a friend, a very gentle and dear friend. It is nice to know that we can be friends even though we are supposed to be enemies. Somehow it restores one's faith in humankind. -

By the time Liesel climbs back into bed, dawn is beginning to break over the mountains of Sarangan, and Willi's face is still there before her... . -'Liesel you want children. You are made for love.' ...Oh, yes, I wanted children, *mein Herz*. And now I am a mother, but you are gone, and half of me is missing. I am alone, more alone than ever, vulnerable, bare.... And yet, we had each other, and we will again! Yes, we will again! I must believe that. We will find each other again after the war is over. It may be years. It may be halfway across the world. But someday, somehow, I know we will be together again! ... If you are still alive... .-

IV

Life had taught Mama very early on how to circumvent unjust laws meant to tyrannize helpless people. She said as much to Sister Agnesella one afternoon, while they were having tea, and I was listening attentively, pretending to be playing with my dolls. Of course, I did not understand what she meant at the time. I was only around four years old, and we were living in Saginomia on the outskirts of Tokyo. Sister Agnesella was one of the Catholic nuns that Mama had befriended. We went to Sunday mass at their little mission chapel when the bombing permitted.

-But what you describe is actually... , well, it's really smuggling, isn't it, Frau *Fiand?- I remember that Sister sounded somewhat shocked but also a little excited. -What if they had caught you?-*

I didn't know what smuggling was, but I remember thinking that it must be something interesting and that I would ask Mama about it later.

-It's a chance one takes in desperate times, Sister- Mama said quite calmly. And then she caught me listening and sent me out to play with the others.

Years later we talked about it again. -Sometimes it is a question of survival; one simply has no choice.- Mama said. - It can be funny, really, but usually only in retrospect. I remember the first time I fooled the foreign authorities and got away with it. It was quite a thrill, and I think now that maybe it is something that becomes addictive in a strange sort of way.

-It was just after the Great War, 1919, I think. I was still living at home then. The French occupation forces had divided the Rheinland *into many little zones, quite at random. It made no sense to the ordinary citizen. We had to apply for permission slips every time we wanted to cross from one zone to another, and we were not allowed to bring certain goods across the boundaries.- Mama shook her head remembering.*

-For example, if you had relatives on a farm, and they wanted to send some produce to their family in town, they were not allowed to do so. It may have had something to do with black marketing, I don't know. All I remember is that we had nothing to eat, and my Tante Maria, *who ran a farm not far from Essen, could not help us. They simply would not give permission for the transport of farm goods, and the family in the city could just starve for all they cared. The farmers were always better off, you know, in war time, and would gladly have shared their bounty. But for some reason that was against the regulations.*

-Anyway, I was always so small and skinny,- she continued. -My mother worried that I was not getting enough to eat. So she came up with the idea that I should visit Tante Maria *in*

the country and live there for a while. Since her farm was not far, we did not think that special permits were required to travel there. So I set out quite happily one morning on the train, only to find out, shortly after we had left the station, that the French police were making the rounds to see if everyone had the required travel permits.

-You can imagine how scared I was. I thought of detention centers and endless questions, and God knows what else, and I certainly did not want to get anyone else into trouble. I was sharing my compartment with a woman and her three children. She must have been in her forties. I remember she was quite plump and cheerful. Her children were fighting and chasing each other, but she was not paying them any attention. She was telling me how foolish she thought these crazy restrictions were and how she would like to give these people a piece of her mind if she could only speak French. When she saw how obviously nervous I was, she knew right away what the matter was.

-'How old are you, anyway,' she asked me. 'You don't need permits if you are under fourteen, you know.' I told her that I was eighteen. 'Well, you certainly don't look it!' she said, looking me up and down. 'I'll tell you what we are going to do. You let your hair down, and I'll put it into braids and pin them up with these ribbons here. Then you sit here by me, and I'll pretend that I am teaching you how to knit. You'll be my oldest daughter. What's your name?'

-When the French police came to our compartment, I was wedged into a corner with Frau Schmitt showing me how to *knit socks, and her children were making enough noise to send the most dedicated police officer running, without bothering to ask any silly questions. She was thrilled with this little ruse, and we had a good laugh.*

-*I used this trick several more times after that,- Mama smiled. —It worked like a charm any time I had to travel around our area. It was an easy matter to put up my long hair in a ponytail and become a little twelve-year-old brat at a moment's notice. There was usually a helpful matron handy to play the exasperated Mama. It was most amusing to find out how much true acting talent there was hidden in ordinary inter-city travelers on a crowded train, especially when they felt themselves unjustly harassed. With time, I added a few frills and a ribbon or two as well as an apron with large hidden pockets. I actually gained weight.-*

*****

Heat and dust and blowing sand. The wind from the sea, warm and moist, provides no relief. Bits of paper are blowing along the quay. People are shouting above the din of cranes, and the ship's horn is blowing incessantly. Everyone is rushing. Liesel's head is spinning, and every now and then, black spots appear before her eyes. The line-up at the customs check is endless. She decides to sit a while longer with the children. When Kaete Zimmerman is finished with her own arrangements, she will come to look after the twins and Hannele.

Everything that Liesel has left in the world, some jewelry and a small amount of money, is sewn into the border of the children's softly padded play carpet. The Dutch authorities have decreed that no one is allowed to leave the country with any valuables. Everything must be left behind, except absolute essentials. The German women and children are leaving Java for Japan, and they are happy to be allowed to leave. In return, however, they must give up the few things of value that are still in their possession and must be prepared to enter a strange land virtually penniless.

The Dutch are actually quite happy to be rid of hundreds of German women and children. They see them as nothing but trouble in time of war, and the Japanese decision to shelter the families of their allies was secretly welcomed by the authorities, though they pretend publicly that it is a generous act of kindness on their part to release the German families. Meanwhile, the women are told that they have the choice of leaving at short notice or of staying in a land that cannot guarantee them safety or even a roof over their heads.

-It is better that you go, *Mevrouw*,- Colonel VanDecker had advised Liesel. - I have heard that your husband and the other men will be taken to mainland India shortly. To a place called Dehra Dun, near the Himalayas. It is run by the English, and they are in a better position there to look after internees. He will not be near you whether you stay or go, and things are getting worse on the islands here. Japan is friendly to you. You will be better protected there.-

Liesel knew of course that this advice was not given lightly. The Colonel was not a happy man either. His world was breaking up too. The war was spreading everywhere, like a festering sore that slowly infects all parts of the body. He had not heard from his mother in Holland for many weeks, and with no family of his own to distract and comfort him, he had become increasingly attached to the girls. To Liesel, he was like a brother. Though she suspected that his feelings for her were stronger, he had never told her as much. On a few occasions, she had caught him looking at her in his gentle way, and there had been a sadness in his eyes, which he then quickly tried to hide with a comment or other. She loved him dearly for his generosity and kindness, and she would miss him.

Some months ago, he had told her happily that a friend of his was going to Atjeh and would take a letter to Willi. -Your husband will be sure to get it, and he can send an answer back. I'll go up to the main house to check on the ladies. You can give me the letter to take to my friend when I come back.-

Liesel had not heard from Willi in such a long time! When he was still interned on Java, a few letters had actually gotten through despite restrictions, and she had been able to send him a picture of the children. Most of his letters to her, however, were strictly censored, and often half of the letter was crossed out in black ink. Eventually, her own letters began to be returned unopened and, when the men were transferred to Atjeh on Sumatra, the correspondence had stopped completely.

Maybe now, through Colonel VanDecker's friend, a letter would reach Willi. Liesel sat down at the small table by the window overlooking the lovely mountains of Sarangan and started to write. -We have your picture on a little table, and every day Hannele brings fresh flowers for 'Papa.' When I ask Baerbel or Resel,

38

'Who is this?' they laugh and say 'Papa.' No matter how long this lasts, the children will know you and love you, *mein Willimann, mein liebstes Herz.* -

One morning, four weeks later, Colonel VanDecker appeared again, smiling with delight. -I have a surprise for you,- he laughed, and with great ceremony handed Liesel a letter. Then, finding some excuse, he left her alone to read and savor her treasure.

Her hands were shaking as she opened the brown paper envelope, and her throat hurt, so that she could hardly swallow. *-Mein liebstes Liesele,-* she read. It was only a typewritten postcard, and the front indicated that it had been inspected. But nothing had been crossed out. It held his love and his concern for her: -How are things with our friends of Sarangan days, *Oma* and Wilma etc? Do you have to manage all alone? I am grateful to all those who may be helping you cope in this difficult time... .-

Here was the paper with his loving name. He had held it in his hand less than a month ago. His signature was there so bold and strong. Liesel pressed it to her heart. He was alive. She had his love always. When the colonel popped in again on his way back, her face was wet with tears, but she was not unhappy. Her tears were tears of gratitude.

On the day they left for Batavia, he stopped to say good-bye before going up to the villa. The children were dressed in their travel outfits, and Liesel was checking the little house for any items that they might have forgotten. He was smiling, of course, as he bent to kiss the girls good-bye, and then he looked at her, and she saw the pain in his eyes and started to cry. He put his big arms around her then and held her for a moment. -We will never see each other again,- he said. -But you will always be in my heart, you and the little ones. May God protect you through this awful time.-

***

-I'm through, thank the good Lord!- Kaete Zimmerman wipes her face with a wet cloth. She has brought a drink for Liesel and the children, and sits down on a suitcase near the twins. -You go now, Liesel. The line-up is getting smaller. But for heaven's sake don't try to smuggle anything through. They found that Christa Braun had hidden her pearls in her hair, in a French role, if you can believe it! Made her loosen her hair right there, and out they fell. Well, they've made a mess of her entire luggage. All over the road! I never saw the likes!-

With sinking heart, Liesel thinks of the children's play rug. They are sitting on it. Too late to do anything about it now. -I'll take my bags over,- she says. -The little ones will sleep on their rug after they've had a drink. They'll be all right here in the shade.-

The officials checking papers and luggage are tired and hot. -Is this all, *Mevrouw*?- one of them asks Liesel, irritation clearly written all over his face.

-Yes, that's it.- Her voice is surprisingly steady. -I have three babies over there by the tree. They are sleeping. You can see them from here.-

-I'm not interested in how many children you have!- he snaps. -Your luggage, is this all you have?- He sizes her up. She wears her hair short now. Nothing hidden there. His eyes wander all over her.

... Do I look as though I would hide the diamond ring that Willi gave me when Hannele was born? Or the pearls that were his wedding gift? Of course not! I will hand everything over to you, you rude excuse for a human being, on a silver platter even, if only I had one, and I'll land on strange soil with three little girls and not a penny to my name!...

-This is all our luggage,- she answers quietly.

-Have you checked her cosmetic bag?- he shouts to his assistant, eyeing Liesel with a superior smile. -Yes, sir! Nothing in the toothpaste, lipstick container, etc. She's clean.-

Liesel leans heavily against the table at her side. She is exhausted and feels dirty and hot. But he keeps her standing there a while longer. ... Oh ye superior human monsters!... Then, with a jerk of the thumb, he indicates that she can pass through to the next group of officials. When she gets back to the children, *Oma* Becker is carrying Resel, and Kaete has Baerbel in one arm and Hannele by the hand. They are talking to a kindly-looking Japanese official from the ship. The rug is gone. Liesel's knees grow weak.

-So you've made it through,- Kaete smiles. -I guess we can board now. I hear the *Asama Maru* is a beautiful ship.

-Where is the children's play rug?-

41

-The rug? Oh dear, yes, where did that boy go with the rug?- Kaete looks about.

-What boy?- the official asks. -Do you need that rug for something? Oh yes, the children, of course.- His voice seems to drift far away... .

When Liesel comes to, someone is wiping her face with a cold cloth. Sounds from far off drift down to her. -What happened?- Her voice is a croak. She can hardly move her lips.

-It's all right. You only fainted.- Kaete is bending over her and, with her, several other people. -She has come to. It must have been the sun.-

Liesel tries to focus on a brightly colored something right in front of her. Red, with blue and yellow flowers and green circles. The rug! They have found the rug! The official from the ship is standing there looking anxious. The play rug is draped over his arm.

-I'm all right.- Liesel whispers. -I'm sorry I fainted. Stupid thing to do. Let's go on board now and get the children settled.-

V

Kobe, Japan, our port of entry after our journey from Batavia, was in the news not so long ago when a terrible earthquake destroyed much of the city. As I watched the devastation on television, I was reminded of the Kobe of early 1945, four years after our first arrival there, when Allied bombers laid waste the city, and the sun was blocked out of the sky by ashes and smoke. And I remembered the mountains around the city, which gave us shelter that day from the worst of the destruction.

It was so dark outside that we children thought we would have to go back to bed again even though we had just had our breakfast. But Mama took us to a mountain cave near the river where our friends and their mothers were already gathered. We were told to play and that everything would be all right, but instead we watched the sky turn blood red in the distance.

I wonder now how much protection that cave would have been had a bomb landed near-by. But the bombers were after bigger gains, the heavy populated areas, and we were safe for the moment, in our little nest in the mountains.

When I think of Kobe today, as I sit snug and warm with husband and children and watch on the news how other countries are being destroyed by new and more sophisticated weaponry, I think of a city that twice played a crucial role in Mama's life – the first was as an entry point to six years of struggle, six years of waiting and praying for this horror to end, and the second was as the light that, as we say, signaled the end of a long dark tunnel.

But I remember too, and with some amusement, that Mama seemed to have a way of attracting guardian angels dressed in pin-striped suits or army uniforms, be they Dutch, German, Japanese or, later, American. There was something about a pretty, yet fragile-looking woman with three small children clinging to her slender frame that brought out the valiant knight protector in friend and foe alike. She struggled along as best she could, until she could no more, and then, out of nowhere it seemed, the rescuer would appear and save the day. She seldom asked for help, but it was offered generously nonetheless, or we would almost certainly not have survived.

****

Kobe in December is cold and wet. The huge overseas reception hall is filled to overflowing with trunks, luggage, and people. The noise is deafening, the confusion supreme. Liesel shivers in her thin gray coat. The children look pale and tired, but at least they do not seem to mind the noise and the cold. Resel has fallen asleep on the play rug. Baerbel is perched on a suitcase and is playing with a set of keys, and Hannele, as always, sits quietly beside her mother, watching everything and whispering the occasional question. They are wearing matching coats and toques, knitted during the long, lonely evenings at Rosenhof, when the removal of all German women and children to Japan was being talked about, and Liesel had suddenly realized that they had nothing warm to wear for a much colder climate. Her own coat is made from one of the light wool blankets at Rosenhof. Thank God for that old sewing machine!

For every woman in the hall there are at least two Japanese officials, counting heads, taking notes, smiling, and bowing. This has gone on for hours now. Liesel watches Wilma Reis arguing with a short, chubby man who will not let go of a large, blue carpetbag, which she claims is hers. He is eyeing her suspiciously and keeps looking pointedly at the blanket she is wearing around her shoulders to keep warm. It has the crest of the *Asama Maru* brightly emblazoned on one corner.

Wilma is tugging vainly at the strap of her bag and talking in a shrill voice that can be heard across the hall. She does not seem to realize that sign language might be more useful, since her adversary obviously does not speak German. Liesel feels a brief urge to go to Wilma's rescue, but then decides she is too tired to care. She has enough to worry about, and Wilma can fend for herself. Her stock of German battle cries is certainly impressive, even if her opponent cannot understand a word she is saying.

Everything seems to be moving in slow motion.... Liesel's head feels light, but her arms and legs are incredibly heavy. She just wants to sit quietly and close her eyes and wait for someone to come along and take over her life. Someone to tell her what will happen next, now that they are finally on

Japanese soil. Someone to tell her where to go, what to do, and how to do it. She pulls Baerbel onto her lap and puts an arm around Hannele. Then she leans back against the cement pillar where she has piled their luggage. She will just close her eyes for a moment.

… The little cabin on the middle deck of the *Asama Maru* is cool and crisp. Their own peaceful little haven. Two big beds, white sheets and a carafe of ice water on a silver tray. What luxury! After the dust and heat of the afternoon on the dock, they all have a long cold drink and then collapse on the two large beds. Later, a hot meal is served in the ship's dining room, but the twins do not want to eat much. Even Hannele, who will do anything to please her Mami, only pecks at her food. And during the night it starts. Resel is the first to wake up crying. Her head is hot, her little body wet with perspiration. Then Baerbel is sick all over her side of the bed. Hannele is next. And this goes on for days. Dysentery, and no doctor aboard to administer even emergency medication. She thanks God that she herself does not get sick and so has the strength to nurse the children. She boils water and makes them drink the sterile liquid to keep them from dehydration. All three are unable to keep down food for days. It is a miracle that they have come through this all right. But now they look emaciated, three white little faces. They look as though they have been abused. …It must have been the ice-cold water. She had not even stopped to see how much the children were drinking and how fast. After the hot afternoon on the quay, the sudden cold liquid in their little stomachs, and the strange food that evening… .She should have been more careful!

Rumor has it that everyone will be taken to a hotel nearby, but Kaete says that there does not appear to be enough room for all the children. She is over in a corner making a valiant effort to communicate with an official who is hard-put to understand her signs and gestures. Everyone's nerves are on edge.

-How funny this would be if I weren't so tired,- Liesel's face twists into a smile at the thought. -How strange to watch this bizarre charade!- So many adults wildly gesticulating. Hands, arms, and legs flailing about. When that does not work, they start to speak very slowly and clearly at first, then louder and louder, until they are screaming at one another. Then, invariably, they stop, look about helplessly and start all over again. -I'll have to remember this scene for some other day, when I'm not too tired to laugh.- Her eyelids burn. They feel like sandpaper.

-*Frau* Fiand? *Frau* Elisabeth Fiand?- A tall, silver-haired man in an impeccably pressed gray suit is standing in front of her. He bows slightly, the better to look into her face, and she sees that he has remarkably blue eyes, which manage to smile and look concerned at the same time. -Forgive me. You are *Frau* Fiand?-

-Yes, yes, I'm Liesel Fiand.- She feels herself go quite red. What a sight she must be! Her hand goes up to her hair. -I'm sorry, I don't seem to be able to.... Do I know you?-

-No, I don't think so,- he smiles good-naturedly. -But I've been watching you for the last little while. You don't seem to be able to stay awake. You are not well.- This is a statement rather than a question, and he does not give her time to form a polite answer. -My wife and I have a large home on the outskirts of Kobe. We have plenty of room and would be delighted if you and your... little family would consider staying with us. My name is Kurt Weisner, I'm with the German consulate here in Kobe.-

There is something so very reassuring about this man. Liesel begins to wonder if he is a figment of her imagination. She had so wished for someone to take charge of her life, if only for a little while, and now here he is, this *Herr* Weisner, like an answer from heaven. But before she can collect her thoughts, let alone answer his kind invitation, she hears a shrill voice behind her.

Herr Konsul Weisner? *Herr Konsul*! How delightful of you to come to welcome us! - Irmgard Reuter is the wife of the former German consul in Batavia. Liesel does not know her very well, but during the voyage to Japan, *Frau Konsul* Reuter, as she still likes to be called, has made a point of surrounding herself with a number of ladies who are obligingly conscious of her former status. She has spent the entire morning keeping several Japanese officials at her beck and call.

-*Frau* Reuter, how nice... er... how very nice to see you! ... Resi... Resi will be delighted, I am sure.... I am just taking *Frau* Fiand and her little girls home with me.- *Herr* Weisner does not even look at Liesel to see if it's all right with her, but stretches out a hand and puts it on her shoulder. - As you can no doubt appreciate, *Frau* Reuter, the Japanese government is doing its very best to make everyone here comfortable, and

I am sure all will be settled shortly. I'll take a run back as soon as we get the little ones and their Mama home. May I count on you, in the meanwhile, to hold down the fort?-

He does not wait for an answer but bows politely, taking her acquiescence for granted, and turns back to Liesel. Two liveried servants appear out of nowhere to take the luggage. *Herr* Weisner picks up Baerbel and holds out a big hand for Hannele, who does not even hesitate. One could cut the surrounding silence with a knife. It seems that the entire hall has come to a standstill and is watching.

-*Herr* Weisner, I must let *Frau* Zimmermann know. She has been such a friend in need.- Liesel searches the room for Kaete and finds her wending her way through the crowd of onlookers.

-Liesel, I'm so glad! - she bursts out. –*Herr* Weisner, I'm delighted to meet you.- She turns to him without ceremony and then back to Liesel, before he replies with a surprised, - Likewise, I'm sure.-

-You'll be much better with the Weisners, and I'll call you when things settle down. Take care, my Dear.- She leans over and kisses Liesel and then hugs Hannele and tells her to be good. Again nodding to *Herr* Weisner, she is off once more, calling to someone who is apparently carrying her suitcase in the wrong direction.

-That was *Frau* Zimmermann, - Liesel explains with a laugh as they are making their way to the doors. A black limousine is waiting for them outside, and Kurt Weisner makes sure everyone is settled comfortably before he takes the seat opposite Liesel. -I hope I was not too abrupt with *Frau* Reuter,- he frowns. –Do you know her well?-

-Hardly,- Liesel smiles. -The children were sick during the voyage over, and I did not have time to... er, ... to socialize.-

-No, I suppose not,- he murmurs, stroking Baerbel's short, straight hair, and running his finger gently around her little ear. -I'm afraid my wife would have crowned me had I invited *Frau* Reuter to come with us. She does not happen to be one of Resi's favorite people,- he confides.

-But.....- You said she would be delighted, Liesel is about to blurt out, but mumbles instead, -I got the impression that you were friends.-

He pulls a face, guessing her thoughts. -Tricks of the diplomatic trade, you know.- He chuckles and shakes his head. Liesel feels as though she has known him all her life, and she is certain that she will like living with the Weisners.

***

Resi Weisner is a woman in her early fifties, of medium height and slender build. Her hair is silver gray, like that of her husband, but her face is round and still young-looking. When she smiles, she is beautiful. She does not wait at the front door as the large car slowly glides to a halt in front of the Weisner's white stone villa, but comes running down the broad

50

flagstone path to welcome Liesel and the children. Her husband smiles and makes the introductions. Everyone is almost immediately on a first name basis.

-And you have a little Resel too!- she cries delightedly. -Oh, it will be so nice to have children in the house once more!-

The Weisners' two sons are in Germany, where they were studying at the University of Heidelberg when the war broke out. -They've enlisted now and are serving the Fatherland,- Resi explains. -They must do their duty, of course,- she adds with a sigh and almost as though to convince herself. -Georg was going with such a lovely girl too, such a lovely girl! But I suppose they will have to wait now till this dreadful business is all over.- Her face looks resigned, but her eyes show a lurking fear.

-Resi is determined to make me a grandfather,- Kurt laughs and winks at Liesel, and she realizes, by the awkward moment of silence, that he is anxious to change the subject. She can imagine how hard it must be for them, so far away from any direct news of the front lines. They are both hurting, but Resi has a harder time to hide her feelings.

-I could not bear it,- she thinks. -My children in danger, and I not there to protect them, not there to make sure they are safe. Not to know from day to day if they are still alive. No! I simply could not bear it! -

The Weisner home is situated on a quiet, tree-lined avenue, far from the noises of the city. The large windows of the two main sitting rooms face the garden, which slopes in terraced sections towards a small wooded area and the sea beyond. It is a peaceful and restful place and, on the surface, the war seems very far away.

After the children are settled in a cozy, bright nursery, with a young Japanese girl to watch over them, and Liesel has had a hot bath and a short nap, she has a leisurely dinner with the Weisners and tells them about the happenings on Java over the last few months.

-This will get worse before it is over,- Resi sighs. -The war will spread, and I feel sorry for any Europeans left there, enemies or not.... It won't go well for them, I am sure.-

Kurt says little, but Liesel knows that he agrees. -Your rescue from Java was most likely the last friendly encounter with our Japanese friends that anyone left in the Dutch East Indies will experience for a long while,- he growls. And Liesel thinks of her dear friend at Rosenhof. "We will never see each other again," he had said, and she feels a tight lump in her throat. -May God protect him through this awful time,- she prays.

Life with the Weisners quickly settles down to a comfortable routine. The Japanese *amah* enjoys looking after the children. They are eating again and quickly begin to look like their normal selves. Hannele is actually learning to speak Japanese. For the first time in many months, Liesel has some leisure moments. When Kurt is in Tokyo, which is often these days, the two women go for long walks along the beach. Resi looks for driftwood and strange shells.

-I always imagine, especially when I see a large piece of wood, that maybe by some quirk of fate this very piece has made its way across the oceans. Maybe it was once part of a tree along... well, the Elbe perhaps.... And it was damaged one gray November day by a wicked storm coming up from the North Sea. Maybe some young boys found this broken branch and dragged it to the river's edge, and when they looked for it the next day, the river had washed it away, out to sea. And here it is now, or at least part of it, waiting for some lonely soul, looking for a sign from home, to find it and carry it up to her house, to polish it and tend it and place it on her porch and be forever reminded of the green shores of the Elbe, and home.- Resi laughs shyly and hands Liesel a driftwood walking stick. - One never knows, this piece may once have been a branch of a tree along the shores of Surabaya. Here, take it. It makes the walking easier on the sand.- Their fingers touch, and Liesel holds her friend's hand for a brief moment. They understand each other.

On rainy days, the women sit by the large windows overlooking the bay and knit. Resi tells Liesel how she met Kurt and what her life has been like as the wife of a German diplomat. Liesel tells her of Willi and their few happy years on Java. And sometimes, in the evening, Resi plays the piano and Liesel sings. It is a tranquil time for both of them. The only unhappiness comes from Liesel's reluctant but necessary weekly visits with the other German ladies, who are now comfortably settled in one of the better hotels in the city. No meals to cook and daily maid service leave plenty of time for gossip. Naturally, Liesel's privileged status as a guest of the German Consul does not go unnoticed.

-What can Kurt Weisner have been thinking of to inflict a house full of brats on Resi?- is a question frequently repeated, as are comments about Liesel herself. -What has Liesel Fiand ever done to merit such preferential treatment? Why she was a simple governess that got lucky when Willi Fiand noticed her.-

Oma Becker takes a malicious pleasure in repeating some of these remarks to Liesel. She makes no effort to water them down. Since tact was never her strong suit, she simply does not realize that this is very painful for her friend. She is only too delighted that some of Surabaya's former elite are now green with envy. *Oma* hasn't forgotten how they treated Liesel at Sarangan, and, although she herself had done nothing to help Liesel then, and even now wouldn't think of standing up for anyone, not even herself, she enjoys seeing people she dislikes punished by circumstances.

Liesel finds her visits to the hotel increasingly embarrassing. She could so easily explain that her so-called 'privileged' status was simply a lucky coincidence, and she would be happy to do this, if someone asked her directly. But, as usual, there are only hints and sly remarks, and she cannot bring herself to honor these with an explanation.

-I was given strict orders by Resi to bring home a nice family with children, and when I saw you half dead in the waiting area, with everyone else running about and shouting, I decided that you were exactly the one Resi would want to nurse and look after,- Kurt had explained several days after Liesel's arrival at their house.

-I told him not to bring back any of those tropical hothouse flowers. You know what I mean. They would want their meals in bed for a month after the ordeal of a long sea voyage, and a maid or two all to themselves to do their bidding. Kurt told me about Irmgard Reuter! That's exactly the type I'm talking about!- Resi raises her eyebrows. - '*Meine lieeebe Frau Konsul* Weisner!' - she mimics. She has never quite gotten used to that title. She was the only daughter of Lutheran missionaries, and any form of pretentiousness is foreign to her. When she met Kurt, her parents were living in semi-retirement near Hamburg, in a quiet cottage by the Elbe, while Resi was studying Asian languages at the university.

-She tutored me in Japanese,- Kurt smiles, -among a lot of other things.- The look they exchange is teasingly tender, and Liesel feels an ache in her heart. She knows this look of lovers.... -Oh Lord, how long it has been! ... Just to see him smile at me again! What I wouldn't do.... What I wouldn't say!-

The days with the Weisners pass quietly, and before long, spring arrives. The cherry blossoms are in bloom. Liesel has never seen anything so beautiful. There is talk that the German women and children will soon be moved further inland to Kyoto. When that happens, her stay with the Weisners will have to end, and she will have to join the others, since, for the time being, the Japanese authorities want the refugees to stay together. -But we'll not worry about that for now,- Resi tells her. -Let's enjoy our time together while we can. In these terrible times, we must learn to take every day as it comes and make the most of it.-

VI

I think of myself as a Child of War. How could I not? Having spent the first five years of my life dodging bombs, running to shelters in the middle of the night, or sitting for hours in a dark hall with pillows over my head wondering what the noise, the flashes of light outside and the breaking glass would do to me.

We were trained to wake, to jump out of bed and into our coats, as soon as we heard the first alarm siren go off in Saginomia, near Tokyo, where we spent the worst part of the war. We slept with our boots on, fully dressed. We would run to the shelter, deep in the ground at the back of the garden of Olga House and there, all members of the large boardinghouse now assembled, we would be assigned a communal bunk with half a dozen other children and be told to go back to sleep.

I don't know what adults think when they order children to go back to sleep after their slumber has been so rudely interrupted. They themselves sat on the wooden benches behind long tables along the wall and listened to the noise outside. Listened and hoped for the all clear "It's over" siren, which often would not sound for hours. They'd play cards or just talk quietly. Some would smoke and, every once in a while, one would get up nervously to look up the stairs of the shelter and ask the watch stationed there what was happening.

I Cry For Innocence

Sometimes a very loud noise would shake everyone and there would be a rush to the exits. The watch would holler that everything was okay, to go back down, and there would be a long discussion about what might have been hit, and what damage might well have been caused.

How could we children possibly sleep? We whispered and poked each other. Small fights would start, and adults would come over and administer a slap or two. Nerves were frayed.

And yet, when I think of my childhood in Japan, other memories have a way of intruding and taking precedence. I remember making snow angels in the back garden after an unusually heavy snowfall in Tokyo. I remember a Christmas tree, all lit up with real candles and glittering with foil paper decorations, and, under the tree, a cloth doll in a green and red apron. I remember a teddy bear and stories and songs before I went to sleep and a warm hug when I woke up after a bad dream.

I would look at Mama's face when all was in turmoil. It was my barometer for danger. I do not ever remember seeing her cry. In all those years, she must surely have wept many times! But I never witnessed a single tear. She knew her girls were looking at her when things were bad, and that our fragile little ship of childhood depended on a safe and steady anchor.

And so the horror, the trauma of it all, somehow did not have the impact on my life that I know it could well have had. My recollections of war, while vivid indeed, are colored by lighter memories because of a stoic woman who loved me.

*****

Liesel is coming back from a long walk by the beach with Hannele, while the twins are having their morning nap, when she sees Kurt Weisner's limousine parked at the front door. He had left very early that morning and had not been there for breakfast. -He must be stopping for his morning coffee with Resi,- she guesses and decides not to intrude. They are so very kind to her and the children, but they must miss their quiet chats together.

Upstairs in her room, the maid is making the beds. She looks nervous. -Weisner-*san* say tell you he want see you,- she says and looks away. Liesel runs down the stairs.

The doors to the larger living room are open and Kurt is pacing the carpet. Liesel hears Resi's voice before she enters the room. -But how could this possibly have happened?- She is sitting by the window and must have seen Liesel and Hannele come back from the beach. Her face is white, and Kurt himself seems to have aged overnight.

-I told you, *Schatz*. They had no way of knowing that all those German men were aboard that ship.- He turns and sees Liesel in the doorway and comes over to stand in front of her. -Liesel,- his large hands take hers. -There's been an accident at sea. You know that the Dutch were transporting the men to mainland India to hand over to the English. Well... the ship was attacked by the Japanese. You see, they were flying the Dutch colors... . I'm afraid it's pretty bad. We don't know how many survived. We know there are some.... They have picked up a few of the men out of the water and are bringing them here by ship. But we don't know how many or when they'll get here.- He takes Liesel over to one of the big chairs, and Resi pours something into a glass. - Here, this will taste strong, but it will do you good.-

Liesel clings to Kurt's hand as if she is afraid he will leave and not answer the question that is uppermost in her mind. -Have you any names.... Of the ones they picked up? Do we know any of the names?-

He shakes his head. -If the people here know, they are not letting on. We don't even know where they are taking the survivors! They are terribly embarrassed by the whole thing, of course. An awful mistake! Bombing a ship with German prisoners of war aboard. Their allies, for heaven's sake! What they really want is for the whole thing to go away, and don't we all? So they don't want to talk about it.- He looks at her and quickly looks away. Liesel feels the blood leave her face. Her stomach is lurching.

-Kurt, for heaven's sake, if you know something, anything at all, tell me! I'd rather know the worst.- She does not realize that she has jumped up and screamed the last few words. Resi puts her arms around her.

-Believe me, Liesel, we have no names,- his voice is gentle. - I know how you feel, and I would not keep anything from you. Please trust me.-

-But why did they not signal that German prisoners were aboard? Why not raise the German flag? A white flag? Anything! There must be an explanation for all this!- Resi cannot stop herself.

Both women look at Kurt. His face is gray, and he looks down at the tips of his shoes, hesitating.

-They have asked me not to tell anyone the circumstances of how the whole thing happened. So please, this cannot go any further... .- He raises his eyes and waits for assurances from both of them. -They are naturally worried about problems should it become known that it was a Japanese attack that caused the wreck. Endless explanations. Security compromised. Obviously hard feelings.... They want to avoid that, if at all possible. They say that the Dutch captain would not signal. The Germans asked to raise their flag, but the fellow wouldn't hear of it.- He walks to the window and stares at the cherry blossoms outside in the garden. -The survivors that were picked up out of the sea say that all the lifeboats were sabotaged except one.... The entire Dutch crew was later picked up in that one.- Kurt's voice shakes. -Our boys tried to hang on, but they were kicked off! God help the Dutch crew, if that is true! -

-How many? How many are dead?-

-We don't know! They won't say! It's a matter of time. They'll send for everyone when the lists are complete... .- His voice sounds tired. - I have to go to the hotel and tell the others.- He leaves quickly, as though to escape.

The two women look at each other. Resi has tears in her eyes, but Liesel's eyes are dry. Her throat hurts, and she cannot swallow. ... -Oh, Willi! *Mein Herz*! How long before I know?-

-He is a good swimmer, - she hears her voice as from a long way off. -He will have known what to do.... .-

***

Weeks go by. Summer is here and Kobe is simmering in an early heat wave. Every day brings new rumors. One ray of hope is the report that not all the men were aboard the doomed ship. There had been three groups of men and three ships. But which ship was sunk? The first? Second? Third? And in what order did the men leave? If they went alphabetically, Willi would surely have been on the first. Was it the first ship? This is foolish mental torture! No one knows anything and the uncertainty is killing. Liesel tells herself that she could face a certainty of grief squarely and know that she must keep on living. But this gnawing fear and doubt! The dreams of waves and sea and miles of horizon. Willi trying to cling on to walls of gray metal and feet kicking his hands. His dear hands! Bleeding! Shark-infested waters! -Oh God! Don't let him be dead! Let me know he is alive! Soon! -

She can hardly stand being with the other women. The forced assurances. The painful smiles. - I am certain that *mein Mann* is among the survivors. -   Just don't look into the speaker's eyes, for she is scared, like you, and hiding from the terror of what could be the truth. No one is certain of anything. It could be yours. It could be mine. And if mine is alive and yours is dead, what can I say in my joy to comfort you?

The children are her one comfort. They are growing, and the twins are beginning to talk. Baerbel is the most affectionate and the most daring. She imitates Hannele and tries to get

61

Resel to follow suit. But Resel prefers to watch her climb on chairs and tables and take the inevitable tumble. She is smaller and more agile but also more timid. -If Willi could see them. I'll have so much to tell him!- But oh! The pain of remembering that there may never be a time to tell him, that she may never, ever see him again, never hold him again , never ever again... .

One afternoon, Resi convinces Liesel to join the other German women for an outing to Kobe's famous *Kabuki* theatre. Complimentary tickets for the German women have been provided by the ladies of the Japanese Cultural Society. Neither Resi nor the ladies of the Cultural Society have, however, thought of providing any information about the play, and most of the Germans take it for a comedy.

Half-way through the performance, a distinct chill can be felt emanating from the rows of Japanese spectators, and Liesel finds herself wishing fervently that Resi had accompanied them to the play. She could have explained what all this was about. At the reception and tea that follows, it is evident that many of the Japanese ladies are extremely upset. They can barely manage to keep up their usual demeanor of polite friendliness. The next day, a very distraught Resi tells Liesel that one of her Japanese friends has expressed surprise at the insensitivity of some of the German ladies who had laughed at the most tragic part of the play.

-How could this have happened? - Resi is on the verge of tears. -I have to find some excuse for this... this breach of polite conduct. What am I going to tell them? They are expecting some sort of formal apology! -

-It was simply a question of language and culture, Resi,- Liesel tries to explain. - Of course, some of the Japanese ladies were crying or at least wiping their eyes. That, in itself, might have been sufficient warning to anyone that this was not something to laugh at. But then again, crying can be part of laughter, you know. It, well... it was just that the whole thing was truly incomprehensible to anyone who did not speak the language. I still don't really know what it was all about. There was this little man dancing about in front of a tiny little dog house. On top of the house were several small tufts of cotton wadding. His face was painted into a frightful mask, and he was crying incessantly in high and low tones of ... well, anguish, I suppose. I thought that maybe his favorite dog had died.-

When Resi groans, Liesel stops. -Are you all right? What's the matter? Was it his dog? Was he lost? I remember my brother Hans had this little Dachshund that decided to run away one day...-

-Oh stop! Please stop! I should have known this would happen! Why did I not go with you? I should have explained!- Resi sighs audibly, but then she looks at Liesel's confused expression and abruptly turns away. – God, this is awful, but... oh dear, a dog house! Oh, my dear!- She can barely contain herself, and Liesel realizes that she is choking with laughter.

-The whole thing was about an old man who is destitute! That little house? Well, it's supposed to be his house! He lives in it. He is destitute! The winter has been devastating. Cotton wadding? Don't you see? Cotton wadding is supposed to be snow! His family has all starved or died of the cold, and he is about to follow suit. He is… , oh, dear! He is saying farewell. He is saying farewell to life!- Tears are running down her cheeks. She is weak with laughter. -Fancy me sitting here laughing myself silly over a poor little old man who is saying farewell to life! - She wipes her eyes, moaning as if in pain. -This is all my fault! Oh, dear me!-

Liesel helps compose an appropriate letter of apology to the dear ladies of the Japanese Cultural Society. -The German guests unfortunately did not fully understand the seriousness of the drama, due to their inability to speak or understand Japanese. They are truly sorry to have caused offense and hope you will be so kind as to excuse this incident. As you are aware, the German ladies have been under severe stress because of the war situation and the uncertainty concerning their husbands.-

-Three tufts of cotton wadding to signify extreme winter conditions? Really Resi! That takes more imagination than I have at the moment!-

Resi shakes her head and smiles. -I don't know if they will be able to understand, even taking into consideration the stress we are all under. It is all a cultural thing, you know. Their view of life has been shaped differently from ours. Did I tell you what I overheard a Japanese mother say to her son as he was leaving to go to war? -

-No, what? -

-I was at the train station and a lot of men were leaving to join up. And, oh, they looked so young in their uniforms! She was standing before her son and bowing, and she said: 'May you be brave and win glory for your country, and may you be granted the ultimate honor of dying for the land of your ancestors.' I heard it, myself. I could not believe it! And then, later, when he had left, I saw her leaving the station, weeping.- Resi stares at the photograph of her own boys in a silver frame on the piano. -They are so different, and yet, they are not! They don't mean it. It must break their hearts. I am sure they can't mean it,- she says. -But they can certainly hide what they feel when they must.... East and West. Strange isn't it?-

***

The waiting goes on. And then, suddenly, it is over. Liesel is at the hotel when they hear that Kurt is on his way with the list of survivors. Everyone rushes to the large reception hall. Liesel tries to prepare herself for the worst. In a short time now the uncertainty will be lifted. No veil to hide behind. Only stark, clear reality. Maybe not knowing is better after all? One can still hope! -How can I keep on living if he is dead?-

She tries to catch Kurt's eye as he enters the room, but he is too tense to see anyone. A dozen voices call out: -Is my husband on the list? *Herr* Weisner, what about my husband?-

-Ladies, ladies! Please! I know that this is terrible for you. I will read the names as fast as possible in alphabetical order. These are the names of the men who are known to have survived. That does not mean that there may not be some men who have somehow gotten through this and may be alive somewhere. We simply cannot be absolutely certain.- His voice shakes and so does the hand holding the paper:

A – Adler, Friedrich

Axel, Ludwig

B - Baum, Fritz

Braun, Kurt

- F ! When will he get to the Fs? Is there not a better way of doing this?

And then she is weeping, weeping for joy. Tears stream down her face, but she doesn't care. He is alive! He was on the first ship. It was the third that went down.

Noise all around her, laughter, cries of pain, screams of happiness. Liesel does not hear any of it. And then she sees Kaete. Her face is white as chalk. She is not crying. Her eyes are like holes, dark, painful things. She comes to Liesel's open arms, moaning quietly like a wounded animal. *–Mein* Bernt, *mein guter, lieber* Bernt!-

VII

Liesel's Journal , September 1942, Kyoto

I have decided to keep a journal. Everyone is dispersing in different directions now. It looks like this might last a very long time, and I have to plan accordingly. If I write things down, even if only every now and then, I'll be able to share this time with Willi, if we... no, when we see each other again. It won't seem like so many lost years. I haven't heard in such a long time.... Kurt says that the Red Cross will take over getting mail to families, but, for the time being, we must be patient. I hate that word!

I really did not want to move to Kyoto at first. But now I am sorry that we can't stay here permanently. I am tired of moving about. But it looks as though we won't be here much longer.

Our move from Kobe was a hard decision to make. I knew, of course, from the start, that my stay with the Weisners would have to end sooner or later, although they both kept insisting that I should think of their place as our home.

Hannele misses Willi, and Kurt was good for her. They both liked to get up early, and every morning she would pay a visit to his study. He would have paper and pencils ready for her, and she would sit across from him at the big desk and imitate him, scribbling endless lines across page after page. Then they'd go for a walk on the beach before breakfast, and she'd come in all excited about the things they had seen.

Resi told me she would visit me in Kyoto. She said that she frequently had business there. It made our parting easier, even though we both knew that we might not see each other often. That's just the way things are now. We make friends, dear friends, and then we have to move on, knowing that we may never see each other again. There is no permanence anymore, no anchor to cling to... .

Someone told us today that Kyoto is the former capital of Japan and that it gave the letters of its name to the present capital, Tokyo. I don't think the two cities have much in common other than that.

This is truly a beautiful place, and we have certainly been able to do a lot of sightseeing over the last few weeks. It seems strange. The bombing has started in earnest, and Tokyo has been struck many times, but we seem to be in a kind of oasis. Our hotel is large and comfortable, and our Japanese hosts are going to a great deal of trouble to make us feel welcome. They have even arranged a few bus tours to various outlying tourist attractions and to some of Kyoto's remarkable temples.

I have taken Hannele with me everywhere. There is usually a group of Japanese ladies to welcome us and shower the children with presents. Lovely silk fans, back-scratchers made of ivory, and little painted wooden spoons to clean out the ears. Hannele always announces that she has two little sisters at home, which means that we get three of everything.

A funny thing happened today. We were visiting one of the temples and were shown a rather ingenious burglar alarm system concealed in a pretty little lacquered bridge leading to the main temple. One can't take five steps across this bridge without setting off, not a shrill whistle or a loud bell, but the sweet, yet quite penetrating song of a thousand birds. It seems the gods ought not to be unduly disturbed even by a potential burglar. While we were admiring the other interesting aspects of the place, Hannele managed to slip back to the little bridge. Well... there was a bit of commotion, followed by smiling and bowing. I kept her little hand in mine for the rest of the visit.

Some of the others are making plans to move. Wilma has already moved to Yokohama to work for a large German firm there. She likes the bright lights of the larger city. Some want to move to Tokyo, despite the bombing, because it has a larger German community. Our hotel will soon be too large for our dwindling numbers.

October 1942, Atami

Oma Becker is here with me in Atami. She can't cope by herself any longer. The troubles of the past two years have been too much for her. She asked Wilma if she could move with her to Yokohama, but Wilma does not want her. She suggested that Oma would be better off with me. I'd have someone 'to help with the children.' Said that she herself has no intention of being 'chaperoned.' A strange way of putting it! But Wilma never ceases to amaze me.

The Mampei Hotel is not as nice as our Kyoto home, but it is large enough for the remaining number of women and children who wish to stay together for the time being.

Kaete is here in Atami. I am glad. The loss of Bernt is still a raw wound. She needs time to think out a new life for herself. And I am happy to have a friend nearby.

The twins draw attention wherever we go. It is quite amusing. When we walk down the street, we are always followed by a crowd of Japanese children, their geta *clattering merrily behind us. This morning, on the way to the barber shop, I counted fifteen. When we stop and turn and bow and say 'auf Wiedersehen,' they smile and, for a minute, stand and stare after us, and then they clatter after us again, faster than ever. I try 'sayonara!' with emphasis. It's no use.*

They stood at the barbershop window and waited for us this morning, their little noses pressed against the large glass pane. The barber was not pleased. He went out and shook his fist at them, and they ran away, but when we came out of the shop, there they were again clattering behind us.

I Cry For Innocence

I am gradually getting to know some of the Japanese customs. They are a very polite people, but I sometimes wonder how much of it is simply show. Much like us, when we ask someone we meet, 'We gehts?' and then run along without waiting for an answer. Only a bit more protracted.

When we got back to the hotel today, after our daily visit to the park, we saw two Japanese gentlemen standing on the steps, bowing to each other. We had to wait because they were blocking the entrance, but they did not notice us. One was obviously in a hurry. He was secretly looking about, as one commuter train passed by and then another, while the other gentleman was bowing and politely asking about the health and general wellbeing of his acquaintance's family, starting, I suppose, with the man's great-grandmother. If your acquaintance asks about your mother-in-law's recent hernia operation, you at least must in return show interest whether his uncle has recovered from his latest bout of stomach trouble, and so it goes on. The twins were fascinated, and I was afraid they would begin to bow to each other.

The two men finally started down the steps just as another train was approaching, but, by the time they actually turned away from each other, the third train was already disappearing in the distance, and the gentleman in a hurry to get to the station stopped long enough to shake his fist at the back of his overly polite acquaintance.

This evening the twins are having a hard time falling asleep. I just peeked in to check on them once more, since I could hear them babbling in their room. And there they were, both out of bed again, little bare feet neatly placed together, facing each other, bowing. Baerbel was making a long speech in some unknown tongue, while Resel, obviously bored, kept up the bowing, looking crosser all the time. 'Me now, me now!' she finally cried, holding up her hand in that rather imperious gesture she has acquired from heaven knows where. And then she started in a flood of words that had nothing in common with Japanese other than sound. I quickly tucked them back into bed before they could start to imitate the fist shaking incident.

*****

The Mampei Hotel is situated near the railway tracks. The front of the hotel faces the station, but the rest of the building is surrounded by a beautiful Japanese garden, carefully designed, complete with pond and little bridge, where guests may spend their time, but where children have little room to run and play.

Liesel and the other German guests take their regular meals in a well-appointed dining room, but she wishes she could cook the meals for the children. They do not like the food here, a type of European cuisine with Japanese overtones, especially prepared for the German guests. Lunch and dinner are an absolute nightmare, though Hannele tries bravely to swallow what she can.

The dining room overlooks the front of the hotel. This provides the occasional diversion whenever the emperor of Japan is expected to pass by, which seems to be rather often these days.

On such occasions, all the shutters facing the railway tracks are closed tightly as a sign of respect for his majesty, and all guests are asked not to open any windows until the imperial train has come and gone. Japanese subjects are not supposed to gaze upon the august person of their revered Emperor.

One noon hour, half the dining room is closed off with beautifully painted silk screens. The hotel manager is very excited and explains, while nervously surveying the horde of German children arriving for their lunch hour meal, that her imperial majesty, the emperor's mother and her entourage are lunching at the hotel.

As usual Resel and Baerbel don't want to eat. No amount of coaxing, warning, promising does any good. It is a lost cause, and this is certainly not the time to make a scene. When Liesel turns to Hannele for just a moment to answer a question, the twins have disappeared. Almost everyone has already finished eating and left the dining room, but a murmur of voices can be heard from behind the silk screens. Liesel has a sickening sensation in the pit of her stomach. No need to search for them, she knows exactly where they are. Those strange screens were simply too much of a temptation!

The manager appears and, smiling broadly, waves to her to come. Resel and Baerbel stand on each side of her imperial majesty, who is patting their shining hair and smilingly asking them questions which they gravely try to answer in a mixture of German words and Japanese sounds. They are favorites with the hotel staff from that day on.

As the days go by, the war also reaches Atami. The food gets worse from day to day, and Liesel begins to worry about the children's health. There are frequent black-outs. Everyone is by now familiar with the hotel's large bomb shelter. The children have fewer and fewer places to play, since walks to the park become too dangerous. To get a bit of fresh air, they must now use the back garden, but Liesel tries to make sure that they do not go near the pond which, though shallow, has not been properly drained for some time and exudes a stagnant, unpleasant smell. But of course, once again, the temptation proves too strong for the adventurous duo. A moment's distraction, and Resel is pulled choking and coughing out of the filthy green mess.

A hot bath washes off the grime, and castor oil makes her vomit, but the next day she is a very sick little girl. The hotel doctor seems at a loss to know what to do, and by nightfall her throat is horribly infected and her temperature close to a hundred and five. -You'll have to take her to a hospital, Liesel,- Kaete has some nursing experience, -I am terribly afraid that it might well be diphtheria.-

Liesel is terrified. It has always seemed to her that if she could just keep her little family together, all would be fine. -The hospital will keep Resel. I will have to leave her. But, of course, Kaete is right. If it's diphtheria…. Oh Lord, that is so terribly contagious!-

Resel is wrapped in a blanket and carried out to a waiting taxi. Her head, resting on Liesel's lap, is hot and damp. She is already delirious. At the Atami hospital they take one look at her and refuse admittance. They have no isolation wards. She would have to try Tokyo. They will phone ahead to alert the hospital in Tokyo.

The driver listens impassively as Liesel pleads with the hospital authorities in her broken Japanese, while Resel moans softly in her arms. She turns to him helplessly. -Will you take us?- He studies her for a moment, frowning, and then he shrugs and nods and smiles at her. Half-way there the black-out sirens go off. No lights! But the driver seems to be a fatalist. Shrugging again, he turns off the lights and steps on the gas.

Tokyo is a maze of dark streets. In the distance, explosions light up the sky. Liesel is certain that they are lost in the inky blackness. The driver curses under his breath and turns sharply into what appears to be a deserted alley. And then, suddenly, there it is, towering square and tall with a hundred black windows, Tokyo General! The driver grins at Liesel's exclamation of relief and helps carry Resel into the hospital. He takes over at the desk and quickly explains the situation. Resel is immediately placed on a stretcher and rushed away down a dark corridor. Both Liesel and the driver are given injections and are asked to take instructions and medication back to Atami. The phone lines are down.

-There is nothing you can do here, Fiand-*san*,- a kind young doctor tells Liesel. -We will do everything in our power for the little one. We will be in touch with you.-

Liesel is thinking of Baerbel and Hannele. What if they have also caught the infection? Kaete has stayed behind to watch over them. The young doctor seems to read her thoughts. -You would do well to check the other children at the hotel. Here you cannot even be with your little daughter.- He sees her face and touches her arm. -She has a good chance. I will call you as soon as the lines are restored or contact you somehow, as soon as we know anything.-

-So I have to go back! Again I must leave you in strange hands, my littlest one! Will you make it through the night?-

On the way home the black-out is lifted. The driver whistles softly and drums his fingers against the steering wheel. In a short while it will be dawn. Liesel sits in the back seat crying quietly.

The hotel is placed under quarantine, but by some miracle no one else catches the infection. The pond is drained, although the hotel doctor refuses to believe that Resel caught the infection there. Everyone receives injections, and Liesel is not very popular with the other guests. She tries to keep the children away from hostile stares and biting comments. These are hard days.

When she is able to visit the hospital, it is a heart-rending experience. -You not my Mami!- Resel cries, holding out little arms, which Liesel cannot take. They've put a white surgical mask on her face, and she is wearing a white gown. She cannot go near the bed and stands in a corner near the door, trying to explain that she is wearing this get-up so that Baerbel and Hannele won't get sick.

Resel is adamant, -Want to go home now. All better. Doctor do bad things. Has big needles, and pussy cat at the window,- she points to the little square of light above her bed, - looks at me in the dark, Mami.-

When she has to leave, Resel does not want to let her go. In desperation, Liesel says that she must visit the bathroom. -My potty here, Mami! My potty! - Resel cries. —Mami won't come back! Mami won't come back!- Her voice echoes along the walls as Liesel runs down the hall.

The next day, a nurse calls to suggest that she should not come again until Resel is ready to go home. -It won't be long now. But she was so terribly upset yesterday and wanted to go home. It is not good for her, and it is an awful thing for you to go through.-

Liesel keeps in touch by phone as often as possible. And then, finally, what seems an eternity later, the call comes that Resel can go home. The danger of contagion is over, and the doctors feel that, since she is so homesick and does not seem to want to eat, she would recuperate better at home. And so, the four of them are back together again and it is hard not to spoil the little invalid. There is an old Japanese proverb that advises the mother to be like a dragon when the child is sick or the child will be like a dragon when it is better. But Liesel feels that they have all deserved the right to ignore this proverb, at least for a little while.

Eventually plans are made to leave Atami. The German government is making a monthly pension available to the

German women with children and, for the time being, they will have enough to get by, without having to depend entirely on Japanese generosity. Liesel hears of a well-run German boarding house in Saginomia, a suburb of Tokyo and decides to investigate it.

VIII

I remember the darkness
and cold
and the back of his head
a dark shadow
among shadows
and Mama's hand
stroking my forehead

There was fear
and the noise of the car
racing
along
dark streets and
the sky
bright yellow and
black and
Mama's hand
stroking my forehead

Or are these memories
only a fusion of sounds
and sensations
of long ago stories told of the night
I was burning
cold
and cold

Theresia M. Quigley

in the back of the car
speeding
in the darkness
and the scent of Mama's coat
like a blanket
and her hand
stroking my forehead?

But there was a cat
in the light
over my bed
in the white room
and strangers
in white coats
and white masks
bringing green needles
and
Mama in the room
saying
'I have to go back'
and
her voice
sounding like tears

My earliest memory
is fear
and
I wonder how much of me
is still part
of that long-ago child
caught in the pain of not knowing
crying

I Cry For Innocence

for the warmth of the arms
that would hold her
and say
all would be well

...But Saginomia is more concrete....

There is a small bedroom with three little beds against the walls, and a large bed-sitting room that opens onto the garden. We have a yellow canary that sits on Mama's finger and likes to be carried around the room, and Sister Olga has a cat.

The garden is looked after by an old Japanese gardener with no teeth and one finger missing on his right hand. There is a swimming pool, but it's empty most of the time. In the far corner of the garden, close to the pool, is the bomb shelter. It is dug deep into the ground, with two entrances, one on each end. Next to it is an old rusty bathtub filled with green water in case of fire. We are not allowed to go near the pool or the green water in the tub. In the back of the house, near the kitchen door is the vegetable garden. We are not allowed to go there either.

Sister Olga has two Japanese maids and a cook. Upstairs, in the corner of the long hall is a room that she keeps locked with a key.

*****

Saginomia is situated on the outskirts of Tokyo, and Olga House, surrounded by a spacious garden, rice paddies and a bamboo grove behind the vegetable patch at the back, has a good reputation among the Tokyo Germans. It had originally belonged to a German business tycoon who, upon his death some years ago, had bequeathed it to an order of Protestant lay sisters. Sister Olga is the only one of the order still in Japan. She has named the house after herself and has recently converted it into a boarding house for German refugees.

-We must look after our own first,- she states firmly. She is a tall, well-built woman, a little on the plump side, who professes to love children. Her rooms are plastered with photographs of herself tending the Japanese orphans who once occupied the home. She immediately takes Liesel into her confidence concerning the problems of running a *Pension* as she calls her establishment.

There is a large, sunny bed-sitting room available for occupancy right now. It has a sun-porch, overlooking the fenced-in garden and a smaller adjacent room, perfect for the children. There is a second small bedroom next door that would do nicely for *Oma* Becker. The food is German, and its preparation is personally supervised by Sister Olga . -I know the eating problems one can have with small children,- she tells Liesel, -and, if you wish, you can prepare some of the meals for the children yourself.-

Somehow she is determined to please, and Liesel cannot find any plausible reason why this is not the ideal place to settle down for the moment, although she finds Sister's overly eager attitude towards her a bit disconcerting.

-She has a way of towering over the person she is speaking to, …or maybe it is just me?- Liesel thinks. —But surely I cannot fault her for being tall. If she invades my space, I can always step back. And she does seem to like the children.… . I really cannot afford to be too picky, and if she bothers me a little, well… I can avoid her, can't I?-

The boarders at Olga House are a strange assortment of people. Some, like *Frau* Wesel, have lived in Japan many years and have come to consider it home. Others, like Else Tonne, have come here, as Liesel did, to find refuge from various parts of war-torn Asia, only to find that the war has followed them and that there really is no place to hide anymore.

As Liesel had feared, Sister Olga makes every effort to establish a close friendship with her from the day they move in, and Liesel somehow feels guilty about this, because she simply cannot bring herself to return the woman's obvious affection for her. There is something about Sister Olga that makes Liesel want to stand back and observe, which becomes increasingly difficult, since Sister is determined to share her every thought with her, including a great deal of unwanted information concerning the other residents of the house.

Else Tonne, it seems, has only one son, twelve-year-old Karl, but she cannot manage him. He has broken several windows already and has stolen repeatedly from the kitchen. Her husband was an overseer at one of the smaller plantations on Borneo.

-He was really nothing special, you know,- Sister whispers. – And everyone that knew him said that he was a brute. Of course, she is not much to look at either. Probably jumped at the chance to get married. But one wonders how such people get together. Big mistake! Big mistake!- she murmurs ominously, and waits for Liesel to ask 'why?'.

Liesel sees Else Tonne every day at mealtime. She is a thin, pale-faced woman with graying hair. There is a perpetually guilty look in her eyes, as though she continually feels she has to apologize for something. She seems incapable of sitting still for any length of time. At their first meeting, they strike up a friendly conversation, and Liesel finds out that Else has been in Japan several months longer than the rest of them, having come on the first ship to leave the Dutch East Indies. As the days go by, however, she seems to withdraw into a shell and will hardly say a word to Liesel.

Oma has heard that Else Tonne's German pension has been cut because of some irregularities concerning her husband, and that she is living in Saginomia at a reduced rate. -That boy of hers is always hungry too,- *Oma* says, -and I think she is afraid to ask Sister for extra food.-

Liesel does not feel that she should interfere, but when she does mention to Sister what a big boy Karl is, she is immediately informed of the boy's latest misdeeds and is glad to let the subject drop. One morning she meets Else in the hall and asks her in for a cup of tea. It is an embarrassing experience. The woman is terribly ill at ease, and Liesel cannot imagine why. When she is leaving, Liesel tells her that she would be so glad if they could become better acquainted and detects a questioning, searching look in her eyes, followed by a momentary glimmer of a smile. From that day on, she makes every effort to befriend Else, despite the fact that Sister Olga does not seem to be too happy about this new relationship.

-I thought you and Sister Olga were bosom pals,- Else explains some time later. -I am afraid she and I do not get along at all. Karl is such a handful, and he does seem to want to annoy her. She made a point of investigating everything about us when we first came here, and now she has some sort of agreement with the German consulate to keep us here, but we are barely tolerated.- She shrugs her shoulders in a resigned fashion, and there is something almost dead in the way she speaks.

-I cannot manage Karl, you know,- she admits at another time. -He is so much like his father, he frightens me.-

-Maybe a little regular discipline... ,- Liesel tries to suggest, since it is her belief that one should not threaten a child with punishment one does not intend to or cannot carry out, and she has seen her friend do this on several occasions. But Else only laughs. A despairing, hollow sound. -Has anyone ever told you anything about Juergen?- she asks, and when Liesel looks puzzled, she adds, - my husband.-

-Now there was a man who believed in the proverb: "When in Rome do as the Romans do," or however that goes. You would never believe any one person could be so different from what he first appeared to be. You see, I met him at university in Hamburg. He was home on holidays. I was studying agriculture, and one of my professors asked him to give a guest lecture on tropical farming. He was very good looking, you know, and oh so charming, when he wanted to be. I fell head over heals in love with him right then and there, and when I heard he had come home to find a wife, I was determined to be introduced to him.

-When he asked me to marry him, I thought he was doing me a favor. My family, my friends, everyone thought how lucky I was. He had everyone completely fooled and me most of all, until we got to Borneo. No, I guess it was on board ship that I first started to feel a little uneasy, because he seemed to drink a lot and had an altercation with the captain. But when we got to the plantation, the lovely villa he had shown me in pictures turned out to belong to the manager. I did not mind our own little place, it was just that he had lied about it. I got pregnant right away, of course, and when I was fairly big, Juergen went back to his native mistress. I confronted him with this. I wasn't so scared of him then, but he told me that we were not in Europe now, and he was not bound by my puritan ideas, that we were in the bush after all, and that we could live by the rules of the bush. 'Everyone here has his little fun. What else is there to do?' he said.

-I wanted a regular doctor, but that meant money. Juergen turned out to be a tightwad. He always had enough money for drinking though. He said the 'bush women' don't need doctors, and I ended up with the native midwife. Karl was a very big baby. It almost killed me. I can't have any more now.- As she talks, she seems to be almost in a trance. -You know, I never thought I could hate. But when those men were lost at sea, and we didn't know for so long if they were alive or dead, I actually wished, prayed, that he'd be among those that drowned. I'd never have to see him again then. But I wasn't that lucky.- She laughs a bitter little laugh. -I suppose you think that's not possible. You think I'm pretty awful now, don't you?-

-No, no! Of course not.- Liesel stammers, but Else does not seem to hear her.

-He turned Karl against me. He taught him to be cruel, actually taught him to hurt animals. 'I'm not going to have a sissy for a son!' he'd say, and then he'd beat me right there in front of the child, if I objected to anything he or Karl did. What kind of respect do you think a boy learns to have for his mother with a father like that? Karl's eyes are just like his father's. He knows that I'm afraid of him.-

Some time after this conversation, Liesel hears strange, choking sounds coming from behind Else Tonne's door. She bangs on the door and calls out for someone to open. Suddenly, the door is flung wide and Karl runs out, his face is red and angry. Else is lying on the couch, gasping, her hands wrapped around her throat.

-Oh *Frau* Fiand, *Frau* Fiand! He...he... he tried to... Karl tried to strangle me. I... I found some money... . It wasn't ours. I tried to make him tell me, but oh... don't tell anyone, please don't tell anyone!-

The next week, Liesel and Else visit the German consul in Tokyo. Something has to be done with Karl, both for his sake and his mother's. Arrangements are worked out to put him in a home for difficult children, on a trial basis. The day before he leaves, he carefully puts a handful of marbles under the little mat by Liesel's door. She almost breaks her neck on the way out. But he is not there to see it, and Liesel simply removes the marbles and never says a world to anyone.

*****

After they have lived in Saginomia for several weeks, Liesel meets *Frau* Wesel quite by accident. She notices that the maid regularly carries a tray into a room under the large stairway, but whenever she passes there, the door is shut. One morning, however, she almost bumps into the girl carrying the breakfast tray. Walking ahead, she opens the door for her and cannot believe the smell that meets her as she does so. The room is dark, and the girl hurries in and closes the door.

-...That room smells like urine! It stinks of ammonia and unwashed linen!- Liesel turns around and goes straight to Sister Olga's rooms. They are large, comfortably furnished, and she is at her desk writing.

-Sister, what is the matter with *Frau* Wesel?-

-*Frau* Wesel? Why? Have you two met? She has been sick for quite some time now.- Sister looks at Liesel with feigned surprise, but quickly looks away. —You have no idea of the trouble I've had here lately.- she sighs. —Somehow, since the war started, the consulate has been sending me everyone they cannot place elsewhere.-

When Liesel lifts her eyebrows, Sister quickly qualifies her statement. —Of course, I don't mean you, my dear, not you, certainly! Why, I thank heaven everyday that you have come into my life! But *Frau* Wesel !- She lifts her eyes imploringly to heaven. –She used to be a school teacher here in Tokyo, you know, but when her husband died, she went slightly crazy. Used to stop along the street and talk to the trees. That didn't bother anyone though. They got quite used to her chatting away to the trees. But then she didn't show up for a long time and someone got suspicious. They found her in a filthy apartment, just lying in bed. She said she did not want to live any longer. The consulate tried to send her back to Germany, where she has a sister, but with the war on, it wouldn't have been easy. Anyway, she did not want to go. Said Japan was where her husband was buried and that's where she would be buried too. They sent her here then, and I told Maria, the maid, to look after her. You know how busy I am ! Anyway…, why do you want to know?- Sister talks very fast and ends by giving Liesel an uneasy, somewhat guilty look.

-It seems Maria is not doing her job.- Liesel says quietly. –*Frau* Wesel's room stinks to high heaven!-

-Oh, surely not!- Sister gets up from behind her desk and immediately goes into a long story of how difficult it is to get good help these days. –And the consulate thinks I can keep people here for nothing!- she adds.

Liesel goes with her to *Frau* Wesel's room. It is unbelievable. She is sure that the windows have not been opened for months. The blinds are down and covered with a thick layer of dust. It seems that *Frau* Wesel cannot get up to relieve herself anymore and, if the maid is not there, she simply has to wet her bed.

Sister goes into a tirade when she sees the condition of the room, but Liesel has a feeling that this is simply for her benefit. The maid does not seem terribly upset, at any rate, and keeps moving at the same slow pace, carrying out Sister's orders.

When *Frau* Wesel sees Liesel, she smiles and holds out her thin hand. –I am so very glad you could come,- she says, smiling as to an old friend. –I'm afraid I can't offer you any tea though. Max forgot to get some at the store. You know how he is! But do sit down! Oh dear, there is no chair. Here, here,- she pats the bed, -sit right here. It has been such a long while since I last saw you, and there is so much to talk about.-

When Liesel suggests that maybe they both would be more comfortable next door, she looks puzzled for a minute, but then, lets herself be carried out without protest. In Liesel's room, *Oma* Becker helps to wash her and brush her long white hair, and all the while Liesel and *Oma* keep up a conversation as if this were the most natural thing in the world. Afterwards, they have some tea, and then *Frau* Wesel falls asleep, exhausted but happy.

Meanwhile, a grand housecleaning is being carried out in *Frau* Wesel's room. The mattress is beyond redemption and has to be thrown out. Sister Olga supervises the whole operation and, by nightfall, everything is ready. Liesel finds it hard to look at Sister, let alone speak to her, but she seems unaware that she might be to blame in any way, and a day or two later, she is knocking at Liesel's door again as friendly as ever.

Liesel now makes a point of visiting her new friend every day and often brings Hannele along. The doctor, who has been called in, feels that *Frau* Wesel does not have long to live. –She has no will to live. She simply wants to die,- he says. –In cases like that, there is little we can do.-

For a little while, Hannele arouses her interest, and she seems to be putting up a fight against death, but then, suddenly, she slips back into complete lethargy. A few days later, holding Liesel's hand, she dies. –I'm coming, Max, dear. Don't be so impatient. I'll be ready in a minute.- she shakes her head and smiles. Then, her hand slips out of Liesel's, and she is gone.

***

Of all the boarders at Olga House, however, undoubtedly the most unusual is *Frau* Sacca. At first the new arrivals do not so much see her as hear her and that by way of full dinner trays being hurled down the big staircase after the maid, three days in a row.

-Oh, that is *Frau* Sacca again!- Sister Olga groans, as the rest of the boarders sit around the large dinner table. -I wonder what is wrong with the food today?-

-If she keeps this up, you soon won't have any dishes left,- Miriam Faust observes, shaking her head. *Frau* Faust has been at Olga House the longest. She has three boys. Franz and Josef are four-year-old twins, and Gert is a tall, gentle, six year old, who likes to play with Hannele.

-I'd worry less about the dishes and more about the maids,- *Oma* comments. -What is the matter with her anyway?-

-Oh, sometimes the spinach is cold, another time the eggs are not quite right. She has bouts when she won't come down to dinner, though she is perfectly capable, you know. When she starts throwing things down the stairs, it is a signal that she's about to break her seclusion.- Sister looks quite apprehensive at this last thought.

-Why doesn't she ring a bell or bang a drum?- *Oma* suggests. -It would certainly be cheaper. Dishes are hard to replace these days, I would think. Though there is nothing like throwing them to relieve tension, I know.- She smiles to herself, and Liesel wonders if there is a side to *Oma* that she has not as yet seen.

-Well, I suppose she does it to relieve tension, or maybe she just hates the world. I really would not know.- Sister later observes to Liesel. -But, you know, I really would not mind if she never left her room. When she comes down, she drives everybody crazy, and she absolutely detests children. I swear that she has extrasensory powers. She will tell you right out that she will not shake hands with anyone, because she cannot stand touching another person. And if children pass her chair and happen just barely to brush against it, she is likely to turn around and hit them. She could not possibly see them touching her chair, but she somehow can feel it.-

-She'd better not try that with mine,- Liesel mutters, under her breath.

A day or two later, *Frau* Sacca appears at the dinner table and Sister introduces her to Liesel, *Oma* and the children. As predicted, no hand is extended. The adults receive a curt nod, while the children are completely ignored. *Frau* Sacca is dressed in an ancient army jacket, green-gray in color, which does not appear to have been washed in years and badly needs mending. Though it is early summer and rather warm, the jacket is buttoned to the neck and, except for the sleeves, is heavily padded.

Frau Sacca's hair is black and straight and cut very short. Her face has a yellow tinge and a leathery look. Throughout the meal she utters not a single word, but when Gert gets up to leave the room, she bites out, -Don't touch me and don't touch my chair.- Liesel notices then that she has quite a heavy accent.

Later, in the garden, while the children play, Miriam Faust is only too anxious to reveal all she knows about -that Sacca woman- as she calls her. Evidently she has had several run-ins with her because of the children.

-She is a regular witch, you know. There is no doubt about it,- she whispers, although there is no one nearby who could overhear their conversation. -You are aware, of course, that she was a soldier in the first war?-

-A soldier? Is that why she wears army clothes?-

-I've never seen her in anything else,- *Frau* Faust continues. -She tried to enlist again this time, but, of course, it did not work. She was younger the first time around. The daughter of some

Hungarian count, they say. Her brother and then her father were killed, and she swore retribution. They say that she was the bravest soldier they had in the regiment. No one suspected that she was a woman until she was wounded in action. They couldn't get over it. She married one of the officers, and somehow they ended up in Japan. When he died, her old regiment collected enough money for a regular passage home. She kept the money and stayed here. Said that a 'von Sacca' never travels any other way but first class. Imagine that!-

-What does she do now?- Liesel wants to know. Despite herself, the woman intrigues her, and Miriam Faust is happy to oblige.

-She has a bar of some sort in Tokyo. I don't know where. It's only open at night anyway, because I see her leave here late in the evening, and she doesn't come back till the early hours of the morning. Someone said that she'd been arrested a couple of times for slapping her clients because she felt that they had insulted her honor in some way. God knows how she ended up here in Olga House. She must be paying a pretty penny, or Sister would not put up with her, I'm sure.-

A few weeks later *Frau* Sacca ends up in jail again, and when she gets out, someone comes to collect her things. The bombing raids on Tokyo have increased steadily during the last weeks, and she evidently feels Saginomia, so close to the airport, is not the safest place to be.

-She knows Tokyo like the back of her hand,- Sister Olga explains. -She will have found a small hole in the wall somewhere, and after the war, there she will be, as if nothing had happened.-

IX

why don't you
write a poem
about war
they said
thinking me capable of
profound thought since
as a child
the scorching "winds of war"
had rocked my cradle

but when I think
of war
I think:
big boys with shiny toys
untried as yet
and eager to be used
with "surgical precision"
in "mop-up operations"
to blow sky high
the bodies of young men
held only yesterday
in arms of tender love

I think
of skies lit up
in a "magnificent display"

I Cry For Innocence

of anti-missile missiles
hiding the stars
that once sufficed to
raise man's eyes in wonder
I think
of mothers clutching
screaming babes
I think of "human shields"
and sanctimonious words
about democracy

no poem comes to mind
only the words
repeated
as in a litany of
prayer:

NO WAR!
OH PLEASE
NOT EVER WAR!
NO, NEVER, EVER WAR!

*****

Towards the end of August, the air raids on and around Tokyo have become an almost daily occurrence, or rather nightly, since for some reason, most of them occur just after midnight, and it is seldom that anyone can get an undisturbed night's sleep. As a result, everyone is tired, and tempers tend to be short. The children are cranky and pale. They don't even try to take off their shoes anymore when they go to bed, knowing full well that they must rush to the shelter as soon as the warning siren goes off.

Strangely enough, when the alarm does go off during the day, it is more difficult to organize everyone to rush to the shelter: the children are scattered throughout the house and must be found; someone is having a bath and must rush into her clothes; everyone is at the dinner table and is trying to grab one more mouthful before dashing away, since no one knows when the next meal will be possible. Often the second siren sounds before the stampede to the back of the garden has even started, and it is too late to make it across the grassy patch to safety. The bombers are already overhead; the whistling sounds of flying metal and the crashing of glass have started. No time to run anywhere.

Everyone huddles in the center hall of the house against the walls, believed to be the safest place, should the house take a hit. *Oma* has Hannele in the far corner. Sister Olga holds Baerbel, who finds the whole thing quite an adventure, while Resel clings to Liesel. The grownups hold cushions over their heads and try to lean over the children to protect them. When a loud boom is heard almost next door, Resel lets out a piercing scream, which starts the other children crying in a chorus. -Hush, hush now. It will soon be over. Just huddle close together.-

-*Tante* Olga, why is *Frau* Tonne not playing hide-and-go-seek under the pillow, like we are?- Baerbel's clear little voice can be heard right across the hall. Liesel turns around to see and there, perched on a trunk, sits Else Tonne, with a steel helmet on her head, eating her soup. Their eyes meet, and she shrugs.

The bombers leave as quickly as they have come. Like receding thunder, the explosions can be heard from farther and farther away now. The worst is over. For the time being, someone else is on the receiving end, and Olga House can breathe again.

-I'm not afraid to die. Why make such a fuss?- Else tells Liesel afterwards. But when Liesel looks at her closely, she adds quietly. -You have three little darlings and a man who loves you. What do I have?-

During the night, the alarm siren sounds again and, this time, there is a mad rush for the shelter. The children are bedded down in the narrow bunks along one wall. Ryoichi-*san,*the old gardener, stations himself at the front exit and gives an account of the happenings outside in Japanese and broken German. Even several feet below ground, one can hear the explosions, often only seconds apart, and Liesel wonders if the house will be standing when they get out. Suddenly a rumbling sound can be heard, and everything begins to shake.

-What is happening?-

-Have we been hit?-

-Look at that chair! It's dancing across the floor!-

-Good Lord! An earthquake! And we can't get out of here!-

Everyone starts talking at the same time. And then Liesel has a thought that chills her to the very bone. The swimming pool! Practically right next to the shelter entrance, full to the brim! They had meant to empty it that very day. It was a foolish luxury in any event in times like this, and no one has used it for weeks. But the attack at noon had everyone so upset, and most of the afternoon was spent clearing away broken glass and repairing windows. Now here they were, with bombs falling all around, caught in an earthquake, and hundreds of gallons of water only a few feet away.

Liesel starts to pray. There is nothing else she can do. -Oh Lord, let us get out of here alive. For the children's sake, who never harmed anyone. Little innocents! Dear Lord, protect them from harm, You, Who love little children. Mary, mother, pray for me.- For a moment, all the horror is blocked from her mind. She thinks only of one thing, if she prays hard enough, if she believes, if she wills it, everything will be all right.

-Mami, you are squeezing my hand.- Liesel is brought back to the present by Hannele's voice, and when she looks up, the trembling earth is calm again, and Ryoichi-*san* tells Sister Olga that he thinks the bombers are leaving. But it takes another hour before the 'All Clear' siren goes and, tired and shivering from the night air, everyone dares go back through the garden to the house, which, once again, has been spared.

-Ask Ryoichi-*san* to empty the pool right away,- Liesel whispers to Sister Olga. -We could all have been drowned tonight.-

Sister gives her a startled look and then turns very white. -Oh my God! The pool! All that water… and the earthquake!-

The pool is kept empty from then on.

A few days later, Liesel has a strange experience. She has an appointment at the German consulate in Tokyo to sign some papers and wants to take the rest of the afternoon to see if she can find some warm material in the Tokyo shops to make winter clothes for the girls, who are growing out of everything. *Oma* offers to look after the children, and Liesel leaves at noon, hoping to be back by supper time.

At the consulate she, quite unexpectedly, meets Wilma Reis, whom she has not seen since Kyoto, and they decide to have tea together. Liesel gives Wilma news of her mother, and Wilma is anxious to fill her in on all the latest gossip in the German community. It seems that several German merchant ships, complete with crew, are presently stranded in Yokohama, and the social life there is quite the thing, despite the bombings.

-Tokyo is such a dull place. I don't know how you can stand it! Come down to Yokohama some time soon. We'll have a great time!-

Liesel smiles. Wilma hasn't changed. -I'll have to be careful to censor what I tell *Oma*,- she thinks.

The last train back to Saginomia leaves at six, and Liesel barely makes the station on time. The shopping has taken longer than she expected, but she has found what she needs, and they won't freeze this winter. The train is crowded and stuffy, and people are pushing each other in all directions. Liesel is one of the last to board and stands close to the door, which is a dangerous place to be on these overcrowded commuter trains, because the passengers trying to get off at various stops are liable to push anyone in their way out with them, and it is sometimes impossible to get back on.

The train has hardly pulled out of the station when Liesel feels an uneasy, almost overwhelming sensation creep through her. Her chest contracts, and she can hardly breathe. Something terrible is going to happen! She knows this feeling. Many years ago in Germany, she had felt it before her father's sudden death and again when Franz's brother was badly hurt in a boat accident. But it has never been this strong. She begins to shake all over and knows suddenly that she must leave the train. They are pulling into the first stop just then. -Let me out! I must get out of here!-

This part of the city is completely unfamiliar. Liesel has no idea where she is or how to get back to Saginomia. But this does not even enter her head as she runs out onto the platform, looking for the nearest exit. All she can think of is to get away from the station and the train as fast as her feet will carry her.

A flight of stairs leads down to the street. It is a poor section of Tokyo, and the smell of burned rubber and garbage is strong in the air. As she runs, she hears the 'emergency' siren go off. Bombers are already over the city. People are running and shouting, and a building only a hundred yards away crashes down in a cloud of dust and flames and blocks the street.

Someone appears out of nowhere and grabs her arm. *–Hayaku koko ni hairi nasai!-* he yells, pulling her into a hole. She hears herself scream, but the man continues to talk rapidly in Japanese trying to explain something, and when she can finally focus in the darkness, she finds herself in a dimly lit bomb shelter with nearly a hundred other people.

The noise outside is deafening. Shrill, piercing screams are drowned out repeatedly by loud explosions which shake the walls of the shelter. The dark outside is lit up by light bombs, and then, with an enormous crash, the sky is suddenly bright as day.

-The station! Oh my God! They've hit the station!-

Liesel feels herself choking. Her ears ring and she is afraid that she will faint. -Oh God! That train! That train full of people! It would not have left, because of the alarm.- Everything has happened so fast. In a matter of a few minutes, seconds it seems, hundreds of people dead! Liesel knows with complete certainty that she is the only passenger still alive.

They've hit their target and are on their way. Everyone scrambles out into the dust and rubble. Women are crying softly. Somewhere a child is screaming. Fires all around provide the only light. Liesel walks for miles through charred streets. She has no idea where she is. Her mind is a foggy haze. When one way is blocked by burning debris, she simply turns to find another exit. People are everywhere, some running, others simply standing there aimlessly, black shadows against a burning sky.

Then, quite suddenly, like a miracle, there is the mission house. Liesel recognizes the chapel, and now she knows exactly where she is. The nuns are out helping the wounded, but Sister Agnesella sees her and runs to embrace her. They take her inside. It is like stepping from hell into heaven.

-You must stay the night,- Sister Agnesella urges. -You must wash and rest.- But Liesel knows that she cannot stay. She must get back to Saginomia. The phone lines are down, and there is no way of knowing if the children are all right. -I have to see to the children. I can't stay, Sister.- Her mind is suddenly clear. -I must leave right away. Now that I have a sense of where I am, I can find my way.-

The Sisters have an old station wagon, and Sister Agnesella insists on driving Liesel. -If the streets are not blocked too badly, this old thing will get us through,- she says. -It won't take us long. I'll probably have to stay with you for the night though.-

When they reach home, it is long past midnight. Sister Olga opens the big front door herself and looks at Liesel as though she were seeing a ghost. She has heard that the train was hit. No possible survivors! -I was sure you were on it,- she cries. -I've been up till now, thinking and praying, hoping for a miracle. Oh, my dearest... .- Tears are running down her cheeks. -You must have a nice warm bath and something to eat. The children will be afraid if they see you like this.-

When Liesel looks into the hall mirror, all she can recognize are her eyes, but they have the look of a hunted animal. Her face, her hands, her hair, everything is covered with soot, with blood.

The next day, they hear that during a bombing attack earlier in the day, near Kobe, a few planes, manned with sharp shooters, had dive-bombed. Many civilians, running for cover had been shot. One of the planes had crashed, and the only survivor, the pilot, had been bludgeoned to death by an angry Japanese mob.

-Oh, this is terrible!- Sister Agnesella cries. She is having a last cup of tea with Liesel and Sister Olga before leaving for the mission, when Ryoichi-*san* arrives with this story. -All this hatred! All this killing!-

-Yes, I suppose one ought to pity that poor man,- Sister Olga agrees. -What a terrible way to die!-

But Liesel shakes her head. -I don't know what happened there,- she says quietly, staring straight ahead. -I know they did not shoot at me yesterday. It was probably too dark. But I can tell you this quite definitely, if one of those sharp-shooting monsters were to fly over this house and cold-bloodedly shoot one of my darlings, running for shelter, and if he then had the misfortune to crash in a field nearby, I would take any weapon I could lay my hands on, a pitch fork even, anything, and I would run to that field as fast as I could, and I would kill him and have no regrets about it.-

There is total silence in the room. The two Sisters look at Liesel aghast. -*Frau* Fiand! You cannot possibly mean that! You could not do such a thing, surely!- Sister Agnesella stammers.

Liesel is very pale, but she nods her head. She looks at the two women; her eyes hurt, and she very much wants to cry. -I'm not talking about the bombers on a mission to destroy some abstract name on a map. I'm talking about men out to kill innocent civilians running for their lives. Children and women running for cover. ... A she-bear attacks to defend her cubs. A cat scratches to protect her kittens. I would not hesitate to kill the killer of my little ones. It would be sheer instinct, primordial mother defending, protecting, yes, even revenging her young. And what is more, I would feel justified!-

They look at her. Neither of them has children of her own. Suddenly Liesel must be with her girls. She runs into the garden and hugs them, all three of them are in her arms. -Oh Willi, if only you were here with me! Just to hear your voice, to see your smile and feel your reassuring arms. How long? How long, must this go on?-

X

I have a tumor on my right ovary. Dr. Winter feels that an immediate operation is necessary.

More than three years have gone by since my world came tumbling down around me, but since that day, the day I said good bye to my darling, in all that time, I don't think I have ever felt so completely alone, so helpless, so frightened as I do now. I have come to think that as long as the children and I are together, we will somehow pull through. They have me, and I have them, and we'll come out of this all right. There have been bombs; we have come close to death, but we were together, and we've survived so far.

Now, I must leave them, and I do not know what will happen to me. What if something goes wrong during the operation? ... After all, this is wartime, and what do I really know about the doctor? What if the tumor is malignant? What will happen to my darlings, my little girls?

I really think war in itself is enough for anyone to have to cope with. Why can't sickness wait for a more opportune time to strike?

Oh dear Lord, don't let me start feeling sorry for myself!

I phoned Resi yesterday and promptly broke down on the phone. She told me that Kurt knows the doctor and that he is reputed to be an excellent surgeon. I did not even have to ask her, she offered to take the girls should anything happen to me. "They will have a home here. Don't even worry for one moment!" she said. But she feels sure that I will be perfectly fine....

September 1944, Tokyo

Kaete came by this morning to take me to the hospital. I made a list of our belongings and left a signed statement as to what is to be done with the children in the event that something should happen to me. I gave these to her before she left me just now. The dear, dear friend! She said that no matter what happens, she will see that the girls get back to Willi when this war is over. She put her arms around me then, and I had a good cry. I feel better now.

Let's get this over with!

...Dr. Winter is a short little man, rather homely. He would not win any medals for his bedside manner either. But I don't care! He told me that all was well and I would be just fine!

Said that they had had a busy time with me, but that everything was in order now. The tumor was very large but of the not-dangerous kind. He certainly took no chances! Took all of the right and part of the left ovary. Said that he left me a little piece of an ovary in case Willi and I want "to have another go at it after the war. A boy maybe," is how he put it! Well, we'll have to see. When he left, he told me that if I had pains in the right lower abdomen at some time in the future, it would not be my appendix. Took that out for good measure.

Hallelujah! I'm all right! Thank you dear Lord, once again, for Your great mercy!

I haven't seen Dr. Winter since the day of the operation, but I've had good care from a young Japanese intern, and there have been lots of visitors. Resi, on a short visit to Tokyo, stopped in to see me for a nice long chat. Kaete comes almost every day. She lives close by. Sister Agnesella and some of the other nuns brought me flowers and Streusselkuchen. *Sister Olga has come several times to bring me news of the children and pretty pictures they have drawn for their Mami. For some reason there is a lull in the air raids over Tokyo, but we hear that Yokohama is having a rough time.*

I have hours to just lie and think...

...How sweet they are, my darlings! Baerbel with her rosy cheeks, always worried that I might be lonely in the house when they are playing outside. I can count on her to come in

to see me every half-hour or so to make sure I am all right. A ray of joy in my room - and, when she runs away to play, there remains the warmth of sunshine....

And Hannele is so kind! It can't be easy for her with identical twin sisters who always steal the show. But she is my heart's delight. I do hope she knows that... . I worry so about her. She cannot seem to defend herself. When a playmate hits her, she just stands there, afraid to hit back, afraid to hurt anyone. How will she cope in this world? How can I prepare her for the pain ahead?...

And then there is Resel, the little one! But I think she is actually tougher than the other two. Maybe because she has been sick so much. And she is most like me... . I do so want the world to be kind to her!...

Sister Olga is looking after them while I'm here. She is very kind to them, I am sure... . But it is odd how a person can be so kind to some and so heartless to others. Sometimes I think she has two personalities. Doesn't like the Faust twins and is forever scolding them for nothing. I think that it's really the mother she doesn't care for, and she sees the mother in the boys. ... And how strange too this thing she has about me. We have nothing in common, really. But she is a lonely woman, I know. Sad really, what she told me about Bett going back to Germany with the other sisters . 'I loved her so. But Bett could never really love me, and so she decided it was better for her to go away and leave me.' There were tears in her eyes, even after all that time. Poor soul! 'But I can't replace

Bett, Olga,' I told her. She looked hurt when I said that. Maybe, I should not have said it.

Doctor Winter came in this morning and said that I can go home tomorrow! I want to see my girls! One can think too much... .

*****

When Liesel gets back to Saginomia, she once again takes over the small *Kindergarten*. The consulate has supplied the crayons, paper, and even a few small tables and chairs. Baerbel and Resel are very competitive and work hard. Franz Faust is a slow learner, but he tries. He likes the color green, and his people, houses, flowers and dogs all eventually end up that color. Liesel gives him a star for effort, but later she hears the twins discussing this apparent injustice:

-He paints his dogs green!-

-Yea! And he doesn't even stay in the lines!-

She tries to explain to the girls that Franz is good in his own way and that everyone who tries should get a star once in a while or else he might stop trying. But Resel looks doubtful, and Baerbel shakes her head and frowns.

Both girls still suck their thumbs. Liesel tries everything to discourage them. They will be five in January. One afternoon, returning from the mission by subway, they see a Japanese gentleman sitting across the aisle. Liesel knows that he is wealthy and does not have to work for a living by the simple fact that his thumbnails have been allowed to grow very long so that they are actually beginning to curve inward. Over the nails he wears silver sheaths to protect them against breaking off.

Baerbel nudges Resel, and both stare at the man's hands with round eyes. They turn to Liesel almost simultaneously. -Mami, look at that man! What's the matter with his thumbs?- Baerbel whispers out of the corner of her mouth. They have been taught not to make loud comments about strangers.

Opportunity knocks but once. -Well, you know, that poor man never would stop sucking his thumb when he was small, and now his nails won't stop growing.- Liesel lies without a moment's hesitation. Two thumbs immediately leave two mouths and are being given a rigorous examination.

That evening, Liesel peeks in on the girls as they are peacefully sleeping. Resel lifts her hand to put her thumb into her mouth and then, with a little frown and a sigh, takes it away again immediately. They both have been permanently cured of thumb-sucking. But Liesel cannot help wondering what Freud might have had to say about this.

When Christmas comes, the little kindergarten group puts on a Christmas play, and, despite the frequent air raids, the sisters from the mission manage to come. Hannele is Mary, dressed in a gown of blue. She takes her role very seriously and sings *Lieb Nachtigal Wach Auf* in her clear little voice, which brings tears to many an eye. Baerbel and Resel are among the angels. They have strong, sure voices and can carry a tune even at their young age. Baerbel makes the occasional grimace when Joseph goes off key, always during the refrain, but she doesn't say a word.

Liesel often sings with the girls and, when she sees how easily they remember whole stanzas and how quickly they learn a tune, she wishes Willi could see them. She had their picture taken and sent it to him through the trusty Red Cross. It has not come back, so surely he will have received it. She sees him, in her mind's eye, study every line and press it to his heart.

The Christmas letter from him, a simple, typed post card, was mostly blacked out as usual by the censors. – But he wrote that he was well, thank God! It's so strange, the magic that emanates from a square piece of paper.... . He has touched it, and now I touch it, and we are joined across thousands of miles.-

Tokyo is being bombed every night now. The children don't say a word anymore when they are wakened in the middle of the night. They simply struggle into their coats and run through the snow to the shelter. It has become routine. Often now, they go right back to sleep on the narrow bunks against the wall. Liesel dozes, her head against her rolled up coat. She is learning to judge the nearness and direction of the explosions, and Else Tonne has actually become an expert at this "game." Everyone's nerves gradually become blunted by the constant danger.

Then, for a week, the bombing takes over the days as well. There is no let up. Days go by when no one sees the daylight. The bomb shelter becomes a permanent home, with the adults dividing into shifts to run to the house and prepare sandwiches, usually at night, because they are afraid of sharpshooters. The children become restless and irritable, and quarrels break out about nothing. They badly need a hot bath. Then, the bombing stops quite suddenly, and everyone can breathe again. However, after this last major offensive, word is received that all German women and children are being evacuated to Takedao, a mountain hamlet not far from Kobe.

Sister Olga refuses to leave Saginomia, and several of the childless residents also choose to remain, but for the women with children, this is not an option. Anything to get away from this hell! Else Tonne hears that Karl is safe in the home in Hakone, and she decides to go to Takedao. She and Liesel have become friends, and she hates the idea of being left behind at Sister Olga's mercy.

-That woman behaves herself when you are around,- she tells Liesel. –I know you don't believe this, but you've been a blessing to this place.- Else is a lonely, bitter woman and often depresses Liesel, but she has a wry sense of humor that tells of the woman she used to be.

-I sang in the church choir at home, you know,- she says one day. -You'd never guess from my voice now, but we carried away many a first prize. I always had a solo part too, but I haven't sung for years now.- She sits there, and a veil seems to fall over her eyes. She is gone, back to her youth and happier days. Suddenly she laughs her self-deprecating, little laugh. –My father wanted me to take music at university. Thought I had a chance in opera. But I had a crush on this fellow in my science class who was into agriculture. He didn't even know I existed. I guess I was an optimist in those days. When you think back, you're always struck by the foolish, insignificant, little things that somehow shape your fate. What an absurd thing life really is! I'd never have met Juergen, if I hadn't had a crush on.... You know, I can't even remember his name now.-

She is an excellent pianist, but it is hard to persuade her to play. - I'm rusty,- she complains. -At Borneo, the manager's wife always wanted me to play at the Friday-night parties. It made me feel so good. I guess every human being needs an occasional pat on the back. But then Juergen told me I was making a fool of myself and that they were asking me only to be polite. He said I was embarrassing him, and, after a while, he wouldn't go to the parties any more, and I really couldn't go alone. I haven't played since then.- But she helped Liesel with the Christmas play, and when the children had gone to bed, she played Liszt's *Liebestraum*, and everyone was amazed at the sensitivity of her touch. For a short while, the war was forgotten.

Sister Olga kisses the children good-bye at the station. She is very tearful. Resel wipes her mouth with the back of her hand, and Baerbel elbows her, afraid that Sister might see and be hurt. –Oh Liesel, *mein Liebes*, do take care of yourself!- Her arms enfold Liesel. –I don't know what I should do if something were to happen to you!- She sincerely means it, and Liesel kisses her cheek, but she cannot help feeling

115

somewhat embarrassed, because Sister hardly shakes hands with Miriam Faust and completely ignores Else.

They are travelling at night for greater safety, and the children are settled on coats spread over benches and suitcases. The railway cars are old and drafty. It will be a long night. Liesel, as usual, uses her coat for a pillow, but sleeping is difficult. She dozes for a few moments, but then, invariably, the train swerves and shudders, and she is awake again.

After three hours of travelling, the train stops so that those who need to, might relieve themselves outside. Privacy is a forgotten luxury in wartime. All this little exercise accomplishes, however, is to wake up most of the children, who begin to cry, upsetting their mothers and causing general confusion. Liesel fears that if she does not take advantage of this opportunity, the girls will no doubt have to go as soon as the train is moving again. She wraps them in their coats and takes them outside. Baerbel and Resel are half asleep during the whole procedure, but, once back in the train, they are wide awake and begin to chatter.

The train rattles on for another hour, and then, with a screeching halt, several people are knocked off their seats, and the lights go out.

-*Mein Gott*! What is happening!- Liesel tries to look through the grimy windows to see where they are.

-Right in the middle of nowhere! We are surrounded by rice paddies,- Else Tonne announces. Then, without warning, the now familiar sound, the droning of the B-29s and, all around, crashing and whizzing, as they unload their deadly cargo.

-Hush!-

-Be quiet, everyone!-

-We must be nearing Kobe. –

-Dear God! Don't let them see the train! Right out in the open, a black shadow amid the rice fields, how can they miss it?- Liesel begins to pray.

Some planes are flying very low, and the sound of the engines makes the air vibrate. Liesel's throat constricts. –Oh please, oh please, don't let them see us!-

The children are watching with big frightened eyes. –How can I hide my fear from them? They mustn't see me afraid! - Her hands shake, and she folds them, pressing them together until the knuckles are white and the fingertips blood red. It stops the shaking. She forces herself to smile.

-Are they looking for us ?- someone whispers.

-Surely they cannot hear people talking,- Liesel thinks. But somehow she feels more secure, hidden in this dead silence, shattered only by the humming engines and the explosions near and far. – How many of them are there? Will there be no end to this terror?-

-They are coming back!-

-They have seen us!-

The last three planes circle around and swoop back towards the train.

-Down! Everybody down!-

-Put something on your heads!-

The whining sound of bombs being hurled from the sky. The momentary flash when they hit the ground. A child whimpers somewhere, but otherwise there is no human sound to be heard. Liesel has thrown herself over the girls. Hannele tries to struggle free, but she pushes her back with the others.

Then, all at once, it is over. Pitch black coldness. The distant, blurred hum of engines and the continual crashing of explosions further and further away. They have another target to hit and cannot waste anymore time and ammunition.

For a while there is confusion as to whether the train was damaged. Someone suggests that they are checking whether the line has been hit. Another argues that they must be waiting until the attack on Kobe is over. Hours drag by in darkness and cold, and no one really knows what the hold-up is. Everyone is talking, and, in the inky blackness, people are falling over each other. Finally, slowly, cautiously, the train starts to move again. A creeping pace, but at least it is moving.

Liesel relaxes a little bit and rearranges the girl's sleeping quarters.
-Maybe we'll be there soon! Oh Lord, help us make it through
the night.-

XI

*My most vivid memory of Takedao is the feeling of hunger.
There either was no food, or the food was so bad that we
could hardly swallow it. I remember being made to sit, for
one whole morning, in front of a dish of grayish-green gruel
which passed as some sort of breakfast cereal. I was told I
could not go out to play until my dish was empty. Mama was
desperate to get some sort of 'nourishment', any kind, into
our little stomachs. On one occasion, when a shipment of
bread finally arrived, it was covered with mold. Mama scraped
off the mold and placed the bread on a sheet outside on the
tin roof to dry. I don't remember eating it.*

*But there were fun times, nevertheless. Mr. Hendrickson, the
schoolteacher, made a bet with Baerbel and me that we could
not bite each other's noses simultaneously. He had, however,
miscalculated, no doubt forgetting the fact that we had spent
nine months together in Mama's womb, in a number of rather
awkward positions. We announced success in short order,
demonstrated that it was indeed no problem at all and
collected our promised yen to everyone's amusement.*

*Mama sang with us and told us stories of how she and Papa
met and what it was like when we were born, and, every
evening, she read us fairy tales. I remember hearing the story
of Pinocchio, and Baerbel cried so hard, because Pinocchio*

had left his poor father all alone and had run away from home, that Mama had to stop reading.

There were plenty of children to play with, and we could sleep through the night, because the bombs fell far away.

*****

Takedao is a small resort community, strung along a mountain stream and boasting, besides the two main hotel buildings, A-House and B-House, and the dining hall belonging to the hotel, a small TB hospital and a "village" of several small huts, made of wood and straw. Across the river and accessible only by a precarious-looking hanging bridge are the doctor's and the nurses' residences. There are no stores in the village. Twice a week, supplies are brought in by train to a sleepy little station several miles away and picked up there by the hotel's mule cart.

Liesel and the girls have been allocated two fairly large eight-*tatami* rooms on the second floor of the A-House, facing the river. She has learned that the size of most Japanese rooms is measured by the number of *tatami*, rectangular, thick, straw mats, which cover the floor and are used as mattresses upon which the bedding is rolled out at night. This is, in fact, how the new arrivals are expected to sleep. During the day, Liesel folds up the bedding and uses it as seats. Furniture seems to be non-existent, and she suspects that the Japanese owners of the hotel, on being ordered to make their place available to German families with children, have removed much of the original furniture for safekeeping. And who can blame them?

However, a few days after their arrival, Liesel discovers some wooden crates at the back of the building, and the hotel manager, Watanabe-*san,* does not object to her using these as substitutes for tables and chairs.

Not so pleasant is the discovery, after their first night in the A-House, that the *tatami* are infested with fleas. The pesky little creatures do not seem to like the twins, but Hannele and Liesel wake up with a multitude of bites and pink bumps all over their arms and legs. *Oma*'s and Else Tonne's rooms, which are across the hall, are not as yet affected by this plague, and the women are only too anxious to help houseclean. Watanabe-*san* pretends great alarm when Liesel reports her predicament to him and assures her that this problem did not exist prior to their arrival. She, on the other hand, denies having brought the infestation to the hotel, and they end up getting nowhere. Back in her rooms, she realizes of course that she should have handled the matter quite differently. Pride is something she cannot afford these days, even when her hygiene is being questioned.

The best solution is to lift the *tatami* and air them outside. They are, however, much heavier than anyone might have expected, and the women have to enlist the help of Mr. Hendrickson, a tall Norwegian schoolteacher with a very nice smile, who has come here from Kobe to teach the older children and whose room is adjacent to Else's.

-Let's line them up here against the veranda railing, in full view of the main street and the hospital next door,- he suggests. - We'll get some sticks and ask the children to beat them with as much gusto and noise as possible.-

Liesel looks at him with surprise, and he winks at her. -You need some disinfectant and scrubbing materials, don't you? Well, 'all's fair in love and war,' as they say. Watanabe-*san* has the reputation of his hotel to consider.-

Just then, Liesel feels another bite and catches the culprit in her hand. But she simply cannot bring herself to squeeze these horrid little offenders to death between her fingers, as Else does, without a second thought. Another method of execution has simply got to be found, and what she finally comes up with has everyone in stitches. Once she catches the offending flea, she quickly spits on the nearest flat surface, window sill, suitcase or the like, places the flea into the saliva and beats it to death with her slipper or shoe. It's a complicated operation, but it works, and she soon is an expert at this procedure, with executions occurring in record time.

The children have hardly begun thrashing the offending *tatami*, when Watanabe-*san* appears with several members of the staff. They are carrying buckets and disinfectants.

-Please, the children may go to play, yes?- he asks, bowing politely. The maids move the *tatami* out of sight around the house and begin scrubbing walls and floors. Miraculously clean *tatami* appear a few hours later and, after Liesel has washed the clothing and everything else that was in the rooms overnight, they are relatively certain of an undisturbed night's rest.

The next evening, she makes her first acquaintance with a public *o-furo*. The hotel has no private baths. It was never intended to serve a European clientele, and the public bathing facilities are an accepted method of bathing for the Japanese. Watanabe-*san* and Liesel have by now resolved their differences and actually become quite friendly. She has worked as hard as his maids in restoring cleanliness to her room, and he appreciates her efforts. When she asks him about bathing the children, he happily shows her the way to the *o-furo* and cannot understand her dismay at finding that she must share these facilities, not only with all the other hotel guests, but also with all the members of his family, the staff, as well as a few villagers, and, what is more, all usually at more or less the same time.

-But it very clean,- he assures Liesel. -All person wash here along side with soap and water, very hot. Buckets here for rinsing body after soap. The *o-furo* is for sit in after wash,- he explains proudly. -Very healthy! O-*furo* is largest in many kilometers.-

-But every one sits here together!'- Liesel feels herself go quite red at the thought, and suddenly he understands and begins to chuckle. -European very funny, very afraid to show body, but hide nothing inside. My people protect what inside, but to show body they not afraid.- He shakes his head and walks away. Liesel has the uncomfortable feeling that he is quite right. -East and West... . We have so much to learn,- she thinks. -We really don't understand each other at all.-

-The less you show your embarrassment the better,- Mr. Hendrickson advises. He has been here a week or two longer

than the others and has used the *o-furo* several times already.
-When I first tried it, I naturally was somewhat taken aback to
see a fat, toothless old lady sitting right at the entrance where I
came in with my towel wrapped around me. I performed the
necessary washing up with my back to her, and when I turned
around to get into the pool.... .-

-Pool?- Else Tonne interrupts him.

-...Well, the bath, I mean, but it rather looks like a large pool, a
hot swimming pool. Anyway, I had my towel in front of me again,
and the old thing had been watching me all the while and began to
cackle and point her finger at me. I got into the water as fast as I
could and almost scalded myself to death. I must warn you, that
water is hot! The others, I mean everyone else there, just behaved
as though the whole procedure were the most natural thing in the
world, and nobody watched anybody in particular. They are used
to it. They really don't care. You've got to remember that.-

The girls think the *o-furo* great fun and, once they are used to the
hot water, they begin to chase each other and even try to swim.
Else has come with Liesel for moral support, and she does not
stop talking for the entire time they are there. Liesel looks at her
as though whatever she is saying is of the utmost interest, and
thus, they both manage to ignore the fact that Watanabe-*san*'s
mother and father are rigorously scrubbing each other only two
feet away.

After they have been in Takedao for a few weeks, Watanabe-*san*
announces that he is losing most of his staff, due to some unforeseen
circumstances which he does not explain. He makes it quite clear

that he cannot be responsible for the preparation and serving of European meals from now on, nor for many of the other amenities he has been providing until now. The end result of this rather unexpected announcement is a decision to form several work details to rotate between cooking, cleaning and serving meals.

To help out with the more strenuous work, Kurt Weisner sends five German merchant marines from Kobe. They are the only survivors of a merchant ship that was blown up in Yokohama harbor some months ago. Sabotage, for which several people are arrested, was blamed for the incident, which caused a great furore in diplomatic circles. One of the marines, Helli Kraus, was badly burned when he jumped overboard into the burning, oil-covered water.

The marines and Mr. Hendrickson are the only European men here, and Liesel wonders what they would have done without the help of the men in the huge kitchen. Cooking for so large a number of women and children is not an easy task, and it is getting harder every day as food is becoming more and more scarce.

-The war can't last much longer,- Helli tells her, when she meets him one day as she and the girls are returning from a short walk along the river. He is a loner and often wanders down to the riverbank, where he sits for long periods of time simply staring straight ahead. -I know you people have heard very little up here in the mountains,- he continues. -But in Kobe, when I was in the hospital there, we heard many rumors. Germany is on the run.- He lowers his voice automatically. -We are being clobbered on all sides now. Rommel is dead.... I met him once, you know, before the war. He was a friend of my uncle. What a guy! There are some crazy stories about his death too. Ah, you don't know what to believe anymore.-

Liesel sits down next to him on a big rock. The children are throwing flat stones into the water, trying to make them skip. -How long, Helli?- she asks him. -How much longer, before this is over?- She realizes with only mild surprise that she really does not care which side wins. If only this would end. If only they could all go home.

-I don't know about Japan. They are determined and tough, and they won't give in easily,- he says. -But for us, I'd say a few more months, maybe less.- She looks at him, surprised. It is March now, surely he must be mistaken.

-We won't be popular around here either, once the *Fuehrer* throws in the towel,- he continues. -In fact, I'd say, it might get darn uncomfortable for a while.-

-Why?- Liesel cries. -Surely they would not blame us?-

-They would see us as traitors,- he says. -They don't like defeat. Fight to the death, *kamikaze* and all that. Why do you think Weisner sent us up here when he heard the staff was deserting? He didn't like the idea of all you ladies and the kids up here alone. You're a friend of his, aren't you?-

-The Weisners were very good to me when we first arrived in Japan. They have been wonderful friends. But they also have many good Japanese friends.-

Helli looks at her and smiles. -He's a nice fellow, Weisner. Too bad about his sons.-

-Have they heard definitely about Georg yet? I know that Helmut was killed in a tank explosion. But Georg... , he went missing at the Russian front.- Liesel sees Resi in her mind's eye, the day she and the girls arrived in Kobe. 'He'll have to wait till this is over to get married now,' she had said. She wanted so much to have her own grandchildren around the house.

-If he's lost at the Russian front, he might as well be dead,- Helli answers, and Liesel suddenly feels the tears run down her cheeks. -This crazy war! This senseless stupidity!-

-Oh, I'm sorry,' Helli stammers. -I didn't mean to frighten you. But you know, it is better to be ready and warned, and things just might get a bit rough here for a while.-

-It's all right, Helli,- Liesel tries to smile. -It just seems such an awful waste of some very good people.-

He looks surprised. -I've been thinking about that for quite a while now,- he murmurs. -In the hospital, you have so much time to just lie there and mull things over in your head. They always want you to rest and keep quiet. I wonder why I'm still alive, when so many of us were blown sky high. Why is Rommel dead? Why did this whole mess start in the first place? But most of my friends don't want to talk about it or even think about it. That's why I come down here to the river. I like the way it sounds so peaceful. I like to think that it was here hundreds of years ago. Just like this probably.

128

And it will be here when we're all dead and gone. And it doesn't care about war or killing. It just runs along on its merry way, making the same, gentle sound. -

He blushes then, suddenly realizing that he has been thinking out loud. But Liesel smiles and nods her head. He gets up and brushes off his pants and looks at her, grinning a little awkwardly. -Anyway, don't worry about what I said. We'll get through this all right. It's just too absurd to think I'd come out of boiling oil alive, only to be sacrificed to the god of war at this late stage.-

They walk back to the hotel together in silence. -What's for dinner today?- Helli asks, and they both grimace. -Turnip soup with rice, if we're lucky, cooked in so-called chicken broth.-

XII

I have started to smoke. I don't know why cigarettes are available when we cannot get any food. My hair is starting to fall out and I've cut it again.

Hannele's really should be cut too, but she cried when I suggested it. Said that she wouldn't be Papa's Maedele *anymore, if her hair were short. It is my fault, of course. I told her once that Willi liked to have a little girl with braids, like all the little girls in Germany. So now she is determined to keep them, no matter what. Even promised to eat 'that awful gray soup' every day and not complain. Poor little thing!*

The smoking takes away my hunger somewhat, and, by cutting a cigarette in two, I can smoke one half at dinner and the other half before bed and save my portion of bread for the girls. I force myself to eat the gray mush that constitutes most of our meals now. Why must all our food be either green or gray? The girls can hardly swallow it, and I find it impossible to force them to eat it.

I Cry For Innocence

May 1945, Takedao

Germany has surrendered! And now we are hardly on speaking terms with our Japanese hosts. As Helli predicted, they are most offended. Sven Hendrickson suspects that there actually is a good supply of food stored somewhere near the hotel, probably in one of the many mountain caverns, and that the reason we were asked to do our own cooking was that our host wanted to save some of the food for this very eventuality. Repeated pleas with Watanabe-san get us nowhere. 'Have own people to feed now,' he says. 'Have to be strong, fight enemy and win! German consul give food to Germans. Go Kobe!'

But the German consulate has been bombed, and the Weisners are dead! Resi! My precious Resi, and Kurt! During the last terrible air raid, they never made it to the shelter. How many more will die and for what? She will never now have a house full of laughing grandchildren. How many of us will be left in the end?

The attack lasted all day, and Kobe is now in ashes. We saw the sun blocked out by cinders and smoke. That must be what hell is like... . The darkness of death and destruction, and hate. Where is hope now? Where is life and love?

*****

-Mami, come quickly! Gert is hitting Hannele!- Baerbel rushes in with the news for at least the fourth time this week, and Liesel is at the end of her wits. Gert Faust and Hannele

131

have always played so well together, but lately there have been many fights, and she can't seem to get to the bottom of the problem. When she goes to investigate, both children just stand there staring angrily at each other, but neither will say what it is all about.

Finally, Liesel tells Hannele that this cannot go on and that she will just have to find someone else to play with. -We all live together here, and we have to try to get along with each other. If you and Gert cannot be nice to each other anymore, maybe it is time you found another friend to play with.- They always have a little chat at bedtime when the twins are already asleep. Liesel finds that she has so little time for just her oldest one, and bedtime seems to be the best time for a quiet moment together.

-But Mami, I like Gert.- Hannele confides haltingly. -But now he always says things that make me scared.- She frowns and seems to concentrate.

-What do you mean, *Liebling?* What does he say to scare you?-

-Well, you know, Mami, the big boys laugh at him because he likes to play with me. They call him a little girl, and he runs away and cries. And then he wants me to take down my panties. He says he wants to see if I am different. And then sometimes he says he does not want to be a boy, and he starts shouting and says that he hates the boys and then he says that he hates me.- She is crying now, and her blue eyes look so tragic that Liesel hugs her close and gently rocks her back and forth. -Mami, why does Gert do that? I want us to play together, like we used to.-

132

-I don't know, *Schatzele*.- Liesel's mind is doing overtime trying to find the right thing to say. -You know, I think that maybe Gert misses his Papa. You are a little girl and you have a Mami to talk to. But Gert is a boy, and he needs a Papa to talk to sometimes. When boys and girls reach a certain age they can get very mixed up and angry, and they don't really know what is the matter with them. It is good when they feel they can talk things over with their Mami or Papa then.-

-I'll always talk things over with you, Mami,- she says and smiles at Liesel, a trusting, loving smile. -Pray God it will always be that way,- Liesel thinks.

She worries about this situation for several days and then, one morning, *Frau* Faust comes to see her. She seems very nervous, and Liesel, hoping for a chance to discuss the children, invites her to sit down and share a cup of tea.

-I really don't quite know what to do about Gert,- Miriam Faust suddenly blurts out in the middle of a discussion about the next kitchen shift. -He is so hard to get along with now. I do so wish that we were in Germany where I could get some proper professional help.-

-I've noticed that he seems somewhat unhappy lately,- Liesel agrees cautiously. -But what do you mean, 'professional help'?-

-There is something wrong with him. He is not quite normal, you know.- Miriam Faust speaks very rapidly now. -I have never told anyone about this. I was so hoping everything would turn out all right. Peter wanted a boy so much, you see. I'd had several miscarriages already. And then, when Gert was born, there was something wrong with him. The doctor said…, well, he said…, well, that Gert could be a girl.- The last few words are rushed out in a low whisper and so quickly that Liesel can hardly make them out and, for a moment, she wonders if she has heard correctly.

-Have you ever heard of such a thing?- Miriam Faust asks and then rushes on without giving Liesel a chance to say anything. - Well, it's true. The doctor used a long Greek word, '*Herma…dite…*' something like that. But Peter wanted a boy so badly! The doctor said we should let it be and see what would happen. Gert should decide for himself later on. It was in some small hospital near Batavia. I don't know if that doctor knew what he was talking about, but you know how it is, you think that if you forget about it, maybe it will go away. Peter's job was not going very well just then either, and so I didn't have time to worry about Gert. And then, I got pregnant with the twins, and I was so sick, nothing mattered any more. Of course, right after they were born the war broke out, and Franz had such a terrible fever, I thought I would lose him.- She stops for breath and looks at Liesel with frightened, questioning eyes.

Liesel does not know what to say, what to tell her to help her. - *Her-maphrodite* is the word,- Liesel thinks. She has heard of it, but she knows next to nothing about such things. Problems like that are hard enough to cope with under normal circumstances, but here in war-ravaged Japan, in a small forsaken mountain village, there are no qualified doctors for miles around, and certainly none who could deal with this sort of thing. And even if there were, they would certainly not speak German. What can she say?

-If Gert feels he can talk to you when he is upset, I think that that is the most important thing right now, *Frau* Faust,- Liesel tries to reassure her. -You really can't do anything right at the moment. Your husband will surely understand that, under the circumstances, all you could give your son was love and understanding. I am sure, when we get back to Germany, there will be qualified help available should Gert need it then.- The words sound hallow. Liesel feels totally helpless and angry with herself for not knowing what else to say or do.

-Yes, of course, you are right,- Miriam Faust nods with a sad smile. -I must simply find more time to spend with Gert and try to win his confidence. I mean... more than he has now. Talk to him, try to get him to talk to me... .- She gives Liesel a lost, unhappy look. -Peter doesn't know about it,- she murmurs. -You know, he wanted a boy so badly,- she says again. -I never had the nerve to tell him. I just couldn't.-

Liesel hugs her. -Things have a way of working themselves out,- she says. -The war changes people's perception of things. Your husband will just be so glad to have you and the children back again. Just you wait and see.-

But after *Frau* Faust leaves, she sits for a long time and stares out into the bright sunny day. -That poor, poor woman! Oh Lord! I truly have so much to be thankful for after all. We have so far survived bombs and hunger, fear of death and sickness, and God knows what still lies ahead. But when at last my ship comes home, and we meet again, Willi and I, there will be no secrets to be afraid of.-

The children are playing outside, and Liesel calls them to go for a walk. Baerbel rushes up with her usual enthusiasm and bumps right into her mother.

-Watch out, *Schatzi,* you mustn't crash into people.-

Baerbel looks up with big eyes. –Why, Mami? Do you have a baby inside your tummy?-

Liesel is caught completely off guard. -What are you saying?-

-Klaus Mueller says that babies grow in Mamis' stomachs. Did I grow in your stomach?-

Liesel decides that maybe it is time to have a serious talk with her little girls.

***

After the major offensive against Kobe, supplies of food stop completely. Two of the marines go to Kobe to find out what is happening and come back with the news that it's every man for himself from now on. There might be the occasional shipment of food, but they're not promising anything. No one can count on anything anymore. Germans are no longer the priority now. They are lucky to be tolerated at all.

-The Japanese surrender must come sooner or later. This cannot go on for much longer,- Sven Hendrickson predicts. -Meanwhile, it wouldn't hurt if we could find that hidden food supply. Watanabe doesn't look as though he has lost a lot of weight, but look at your girls!- He does not realize how much this comment hurts Liesel. Resel and Baerbel are standing there on spindly legs, their round little faces have become thin and white.

-We'll have to organize search parties,- Else Tonne suggests, suddenly very interested in what might turn out to be a bit of an adventure. -But we have to be very careful. It can't look as though we are searching for anything. -

Helli is immediately interested, and several of the marines, who often go climbing behind the hotel, are enlisted as well. On their daily walks, Liesel encourages the children to explore the woods which border the narrow road. -Let's see if we can find some hidden caves. Who knows, there might be pirate treasure no one has found yet.-

When Watanabe-*san* sees the girls on one of their expeditions in the woods nearby and asks them rather crossly what they are doing, Hannele tells him proudly that they are looking for pirate gold. He shakes his head and walks away. But the next day, like a miracle from heaven, the pirate treasure actually materializes. Helli and Sven Hendrickson come to Liesel's room grinning from ear to ear.

-He's got it hidden in an old shed down by the river. I always thought that it was an old abandoned outhouse. But I've been spying on them for a week now, and yesterday, I saw old Watanabe himself go down there late in the evening and come back with a bag of something.- Helli has turned red with excitement. -I stole down to the shed this evening, while they were having their supper. It was locked solid. Sven and I went down again after dark with a screwdriver and a flashlight. The place is full of cans of food. I don't know how he could have accumulated so much, but I wouldn't be surprised if much of it came from our former Kobe supplies. He was always so anxious to make the pickups at the railway station by himself. Anyway, you should see our rooms… , and it didn't even make a dent in his supplies.-

-Good God! What if he finds out? - Else cries with alarm. But Sven laughs reassuringly. -I wouldn't worry about it, Else,- he says kindly and makes her blush. It is the first time Liesel has heard him use her given name, and Else looks away quickly when their eyes meet. She tries so hard to appear cool and aloof when Sven is with them, but he always manages to shatter her forced calmness. Liesel suspects he does it on purpose and wonders why. She has seen them walking together by the river, and once, quite unexpectedly, she came upon them sitting on Helli's rock, her hand in his.

-We'll be careful, but we have to have food, and there is enough for us all. Now we can add some meat to that mush at dinner, and if anyone asks, we'll explain that an unexpected shipment has arrived which has to be strictly rationed. We'll let the fellows in the kitchen know about our little discovery, but not where we found it. The fewer that know, the better. When we run out, we'll pay another night visit to the "outhouse."-

-But how long before they find out?- Else insists.

-We'll worry about that if it happens, and they'll have to catch us first. We took the tins from the back of the pile. Judging by how dusty they were, Watanabe hasn't looked for those for some time. Tonight, we are digging a hole in the woods and putting our loot in there. He might eventually suspect us, but he won't be able to prove it. He is not the only one who can put on an act.- Sven grins, looking much like a schoolboy who has gotten away with playing hookey.

Helli nods. -I'm convinced the food is ours,- he says. -But, of course, the cans are not marked. Watanabe was just looking out for his own people, and now, so are we. We can always say that we had the foresight of storing food away for emergencies like now.-

The food situation improves, but the bad feelings do not, as the war continues to go badly for the Japanese. The Watanabes completely ignore their now unwelcome German guests, and some of the villagers turn their backs when Liese goes by with the girls. Helli reports a second padlock on the storage shed. -It's a good thing they taught us a few useful tricks in the merchant marines,- he grins. With the more nourishing food, spirits rise, and mealtimes become once again a more pleasant event. The weather is warm and sunny, and the children have the energy to chase each other around the compound.

And then, August 6, Hiroshima! And all laughter dies!

-They've dropped some sort of super bomb!- Sven's voice is shaking. -Hundreds of thousands of people are dead for miles around! Thousands more are burned beyond recognition!- He is

139

very pale. Liesel has never seen him so upset. She doesn't know where he gets his information, but it always seems to be correct. Else tells her that she thinks he has some sort of illegal radio setup in his room. And, by now, Liesel feels that Else would know rather than merely suspect such a thing.

-If Hirohito does not step in right away to end this, we are in for a lot of trouble!- Pearls of perspiration trickle down Sven's forehead, and he wipes them away impatiently. -*Frau* Fiand, there are people who are saying that unless the Emperor acts now, we may all die. There is so much terrible bitterness.-

-Oh, come now! Surely… -

-Please, listen to me!- He lifts a shaky hand and looks at Liesel, but his eyes see other things, horrible things. -At times like this, anything is possible. I've come to give you these,- he says, holding out a small bottle of white pills. -Here, take them, in case worse comes to worse. Give one each to the children. They are painless and quick.- He thrusts the bottle into Liesel's hand and, for a moment, focusing all his energy on her, he says firmly, -Don't throw them away! Keep them in a safe place. You might need them.- He leaves the room quickly, and she sees him knocking on Else's door.

Liesel is stunned. She hears the girls downstairs in the garden. They are playing hide-and-go-seek. She looks at Willi's picture standing on a small wooden crate with a glass of fresh wild flowers, and she starts to cry. Years of fear and a lifetime of yearning well up inside and gush out in torrents. *Oma* finds her huddled in a corner, clutching the little bottle of pills, sobbing.

140

-Come Liesel, come. It will be all right. We've been through so much already. Pull yourself together, Liesel. What if the children should find you like this?-

-The children.... Yes, the children. I must get up and wash my face. This is all nonsense, of course. How foolish! I... I am sorry, *Oma*.- Liesel gets up to bathe her face in a bowl of cold water. But before she does, she slips the little bottle into her purse.

XIII

I was sitting on the front steps of A-House when it happened. Mama was upstairs in our rooms, sewing, and Baerbel and Hannele were playing with friends in B-House. It was hot. I remember watching the leaves of the large maple in front of the house, and not one of them was moving. A large, brown toad was hiding in the shade under the house. Everything was very quiet. And then I heard a shout and someone running down the flight of stairs behind me. It was Mr. Hendrickson.

-Where is your Mama?- he asked me, as he was running by. - Quickly, Resel, call your Mama and Oma *Becker . We have some wonderful news. Tell everyone to come to the dining hall, hurry!- He was shouting the same thing to someone walking by, and when I came back with Mama and* Oma *behind me, I saw people running from everywhere towards the dining hall. By the time we got there, the room was already crowded, and Mr. Hendrickson was standing on a chair, waving his arms for silence.*

-I've just heard the news on the radio. The Emperor Hirohito. It's all over! Finally, it's over! The Emperor has surrendered in the name of the Japanese nation! It is an unconditional surrender. He said that in the last week hundreds of thousands of his people have died, first in Hiroshima and then in

Nagasaki. 'There must be an end to this bloodshed,' he said. The first Americans have already landed. The war is over!-

Everyone is assembled in the one large room of the compound, but there is not a sound to be heard. Total silence, and people staring at each other. And then one voice, loud and clear, starts singing: 'Grosser Gott wir loben Dich.' *And within seconds the hall is filled with voices, singing and crying at the same time.* 'Holy God We Praise Thy Name.' *The war is finally over!*

And then they all start laughing and hugging each other, and I am confused. But Mama holds me close, and everyone is shaking hands and talking in loud, happy voices. -Dawn has broken, and the birds are singing again,- Frau *Tonne whispers, and she is crying. And I listen for the birds and wonder why she is crying.*

Since that day, I have seen many newsreels and movies depicting that eventful day. The singing in the streets, the tears and the rejoicing all over the world. The "Hun" had been crushed. The "Jap" had been ground into the dust. Terror and inhumanity would reign no more. The war of all wars had been fought and won! But each time, all I can see in my mind's eye is a little village, high in the mountains outside of Kobe, and a hundred women and children, mothers, wives, lovers, relatives and friends of the vanquished foe, crying for joy and praying in thanksgiving

*****

During the days that followed the atom bombs on Hiroshima and Nagasaki, Liesel and the children hardly left the house. The general consensus was that keeping out of sight as much as possible would probably be the wisest thing under the circumstances. Everyone was restricted to the compound, and noise was kept to a minimum. But even now, a few short days later, with the war officially over, no one quite knows what to expect. How long would they be staying in Takedao? Indeed, would anyone remember that they were here? After the initial euphoria, worries set in.

There is very little news. No fresh food supplies whatsoever, no mail. It seems as though Takedao has been cut off from the rest of the world. One good thing - not long after the surrender , Watanabe-*san* comes to see Liesel and hands over a key to the storage shed, making night forays no longer necessary. He also offers help with some of the chores around the hotel compound. No one quite knows why, but everyone is glad the tension seems to have eased, and the remaining food is now shared openly.

Eventually, however, with food stocks reaching a dangerously low level, something must be done to alert the authorities of the situation in Takedao, and Sven Hendrickson volunteers to go to Kobe to speak to the Americans, who have by now taken control of the country. He speaks English fluently, was never actively involved in the war, and is a Norwegian rather than a German. -I'll speak to someone in charge, never fear,- he promises cheerfully. -They will at least find out that we are here and that we need food.-

Since the railway has not been operating for some time, he will have to walk. Helli agrees to go along to keep him company.

-I hope they will be all right.- Else Tonne murmurs as she and Liesel watch the two men disappear around a distant bend in the road. -I might as well tell you, Liesel, because you probably have guessed by now anyway. I love him, and he loves me.- She does not look at Liesel but keeps staring in the direction of Kobe. -He knows all about Juergen and Karl, of course, but he says it does not matter. You know, at first, I wouldn't admit that I could love again. I've been a fool so many times, and I rushed into my marriage with Juergen like the silly, romantic schoolgirl that I was. I can't afford any more mistakes.- She turns to look at Liesel, anxious for approval. They are walking along the river and finally sit down on Helli's rock, where she had seen them together some time ago.

-You are hardly a romantic schoolgirl now, Else,- Liesel replies gently.

-Yes, but I was so frightened. You know, I had forgotten what tenderness, gentleness in love could be. Or maybe I never really knew. It is so long ago since Juergen courted me in Germany, and even then, he did not mean it, and it was never like this. Sven is oh... oh, so...well, kind, you know. He actually thinks of *me*. He worries whether I am ... well..., fulfilled.- She blushes and looks away.

-We make love, of course,- she says, trying to sound casual about it. -Not at first, though.... I just couldn't. I pretended that I did not want it, did not need it. He never pressured me, you know. I told him once that I would never love again, that we must just be good friends. So we would talk about music. He loves Brahms. Or about books. He would tease me sometimes, in a gentle sort of way, when I tried to be so calm and cool. But then one day, I knew that I needed him as much as he needed me, and he was there, and it just happened, and it was wonderful! - There are tears in her eyes now.

Liesel feels a wave of longing that hurts unbearably. -Oh God! To be loved again!- But her voice sounds steady enough. -What will you do about Karl and Juergen? You say that Sven knows all about them. Have you decided anything definite?-

-Sven says he would look after Karl, if Karl wants to be with us. He is a schoolteacher, and he has had experience with difficult children, you know. But I think Karl might want to be with his father.... I have not seen him now for such a long time, and there has been no mail. I wonder sometimes if he even thinks of me.- She drifts into thought, and Liesel lets her be. They sit side by side, each in a different world of thoughts and memories.

-I will get a divorce from Juergen as soon as that is possible,- Else says suddenly. Her voice is quiet and determined. Gone is the frightened, haggard-looking woman of Saginomia. -It might be years from now. Lord knows when we can get back to Germany. But I know that Sven loves me, and we will be married some day.- She shows Liesel a small university signet ring, the type that men wear on their little fingers. She is wearing it on a gold chain around her neck.

-It's my wedding band until we can get a real one,- she says proudly. - Sven says that marriage is a contract of love. But Juergen never really loved me. He needed a wife, a status symbol, someone to give him a son and wash his dirty clothes.

And so, I think there maybe really never was a marriage, a true marriage, I mean. But now, I feel loved, and I love and, you know, I feel married.-

Liesel nods and puts an arm around her friend. What can she say? War destroys so many marriages. She thinks of Wilma, who is having the time of her life, while her Hans is lingering in a concentration camp somewhere near the Himalayas in India. And she is just one example. There are countless other women and men like her. Loyalty, fidelity sometimes seem the exception rather than the rule. But is Else not right? Her marriage to Juergen had destroyed her, made her a shadow of her former self, a frightened, trembling woman. Now she is whole again and happy, and Liesel can only be happy for her.

As they go back to the house, Else tells her that Sven's parents have a small farm in Norway and that he plans to go back there as soon as they both are able to leave Japan.

-He says that he will not leave without me, and that he will help me see this thing through with Juergen.- Then she laughs. -You know, I was thinking, maybe it is a good thing after all that I studied agriculture at college. Isn't life funny!-

When the men come back from Kobe, the news is not good. It looks as though no one will be leaving Takedao for several more months, if not longer.

-It took me two whole days to get in to see the American commander in charge,- Sven reports. He looks tired and discouraged. -The line outside his door was a mile long, and

147

everyone had an emergency of some kind. They are still trying to get organized in Kobe. The commander thought I was out of my mind to suggest transportation out of here. 'What's wrong with the place?' he wanted to know. 'I hear the fishing up there is something else!' I told him that that was news to me and that we had been on the brink of starvation for the last six months; that the houses had been built for summer occupancy and that a winter there could be catastrophic, because the women and children simply had no reserves left to fight any kind of cold, and we had no medicine whatsoever to help them.

-He hardly listened to me. Said we had a roof over our heads and that was more than most had. And, God! When you see Kobe, you have to believe him! Then he started about fishing again and how he and his father had gone up to Canada each year to salmon fish. I'm afraid I did not show much interest in his anecdotes. I was about ready to choke the fellow. Anyway, he suddenly remembered all the people outside waiting to see him and said he'd see what he could do. They were restoring the railway and would be sending provisions up shortly. I made sure he had that down on a piece of paper or he probably would have forgotten it the minute I left. He also promised that if they had camps set up in time, they'd try to get us out before the snow hits the mountains.- Sven shakes his head frowning, and Helli looks at the floor and shuffles his feet uncomfortably.

-Well, Kobe is a mess,- he mumbles. -I guess we can't expect to be first priority with them, and they did promise food. So we'll just have to make do with that for the time being.-

Both men feel that they have let down their friends in need, but Liesel tells them it was foolish, under the circumstances, to have expected everything to be straightened out in short order. -Let's stop brooding and start organizing some activities that will keep everybody busy and reasonably happy,- she suggests briskly.

Sven and Else agree to reorganize classes for the older children. School hours had been sadly neglected during the days before the surrender. Since there are no blackboards and very few pencils, Sven spends class time telling stories about his many trips to all parts of the world. History too is a specialty, and he makes it as interesting as possible through stories and songs, so that he has no difficulty with truancy. Else takes the children on field trips to explore the flora and fauna of the area, and Liesel wishes that the twins were a little older and could partake in these activities. But there are too many older children, and Resel and Baerbel attend the less popular morning sessions with *Oma* Becker and Miriam Faust, who have agreed to look after the smaller children.

Helli decides to see whether the American commander was right about the fishing in the area. No one can recall ever seeing anyone fish around the hotel, and there is no fishing tackle to be found anywhere on the premises. After a few days of unsuccessfully trying to lure fish out of the river with a home-made apparatus, he takes a walk into the village to see what he can find there. There had been so much bad feeling on both sides during the final days of the war, that few of the Germans even now venture into the village without good reason, fearing that they are now being suspected of collaboration with the oppressor - the occupation forces.

Helli's sign language and few words of Japanese meet with little success. The men simply look at him and shrug their shoulders, and the women smile, with their hands in front of their mouths. Liesel suggests that, the next time, he should take a couple of the small boys along, because most of the children speak some Japanese, but mainly because children hold a particular place in Japanese beliefs and mythology.

She had found this out during her first weeks in Tokyo. The subway trains there were invariably crowded to the hilt and seating accommodations were usually at a minimum. When she traveled with the children, however, she was almost always assured of a seat. They would make their way ahead of her into the crowded car, and immediately, several gentlemen would get up to allow them to sit. They would, of course, accept the seats with a polite '*domo arigato*' and then one of them would jump up for Liesel and sit on her lap. This was not always looked upon favorably. The gentlemen had given their seats to the children, not to a foreign woman.

The whole thing was brought to a head one day when a Japanese gentleman, seated comfortably, while a very pregnant woman was standing in front of him, got up to give his seat to Hannele. Liesel told Hannele to thank the kind gentleman and then offered the seat to the pregnant woman, who looked exceedingly tired and gratefully, but with obvious surprise, accepted the seat. The man was so annoyed that he began to scold Liesel in a loud voice and then, shaking his head and mumbling furiously, made his way to the front of the car.

When Liesel mentioned this incident to Sister Agnesella a few days later, she smiled and nodded. -The Japanese family is divided into a strict hierarchy,- she explained. - First and foremost, there is the grandmother. She wields extraordinary power in the household, and many a young bride is rather frightened of her mother-in-law. Then there is, of course, the husband, and very last and least comes the wife. The children, however, hold a special place. Many of the older Japanese believe that if they are unkind to a child, the child might possibly die because of this unkindness, and then the ghost of that child would come to haunt them and never again give them peace.-

This was valuable information to have in crisis situations, and Liesel did not hesitate to put it to use on several occasions when she needed supplies which would otherwise have been denied her. All she had to do was take the children with her to a store and, after only a moment's hesitation, the shopkeeper would smile and nod and sell her what she needed.

Helli decides to give it a try and heads back to the village, surrounded by a group of boys, each holding a stick and a piece of string. Gert speaks Japanese more fluently than the others and explains to a group of older men, who are sunning themselves in front of a small house, that he and his friends would like to go fishing, but that the river in front of the hotel does not seem to be a good place at all. The men grin at him, and one toothless old fellow examines his crude equipment.

-We do not fish near the hotel and the hospital. There are only a few fish there and they are no good,- he explains in Japanese. He pulls a face and then points in the direction up stream. -There is a big dam with many fish. Very good, big fish.- When Gert points to his fishing tackle, however, the men once again pretend they do not understand a word and only smile and nod.

The next day, Helli, two of the other marines and several boys set out on a day-long fishing excursion. It is late September now, but still warm and sunny. The boys are enthusiastic and hopeful, and Liesel wishes she could go with them. The dam is at least five miles from the village, according to Watanabe-*san*, and the men have packed a good lunch. For once, there is no need to ration. Tonight everyone will have fresh fish to eat.

-There is nothing better than a feed of fresh trout,- *Oma* Becker states, as the women wave good-bye to the fishermen. -But I wouldn't set my heart on it. Have you seen Helli fish? A clumsier fellow I never laid eyes on! But he is so optimistic, and he means so well, one really hates to disillusion him.-

Else laughs. -He's told the kitchen to plan on a weekly feed of fish from now on,- she says.

Come suppertime, there is still no sign of the little band. Some of the mothers are beginning to worry. Finally, as it is getting dark, a straggly-looking band of tired, dusty, hungry, and empty-handed fishermen troop into the yard.

-It was the equipment!-

-Aw, go on! There weren't any fish there!-

-Yes, there were so. I had a big one, but Klaus pushed me, and it got away from me.-

-It didn't like the worm you had on the line.-

-You never had anything bite except an eel.-

It does not take long before the boys are rolling in the dust punching each other. The men look sheepish.

-I guess we can put that down as an experiment that failed.- Helli grumbles. But *Oma* smiles and asks, -Did you have fun?-

-Well, yes! At first anyway. But we sure hated to come home without any fish.- Helli admits.

-Well, as long as you had a good time, it was worth it,- she says. -I don't think even the best fisherman could have done much with a stick and a clothesline. But it was a lovely day, and you had fun. After so much misery for the last months, you all deserved a holiday anyway.- That settles it, and Liesel smiles at *Oma*'s occasional flashes of wisdom. Pretty soon everyone is being regaled with stories of fun and adventure, and the fish that would not bite are quickly forgotten.

The Americans are true to their word and send the occasional shipment of supplies, which is dutifully shared with the Watanabes. Takedao in autumn is a mass of color, and Liesel sometimes catches herself thinking that life here is not so bad after all, and, at any rate, vastly preferable to an army camp.

XIV

When I remember the round about way Mama had of killing fleas, it is hard to believe that she became known as 'the number one snake destroyer of Takedao.' The place was infested with the creatures, and none of the marines nor any of the women would have anything to do with them if they could help it.

Mama had been told by the gardener in Surabaya that one way of distinguishing a poisonous snake from a non-poisonous one was by the shape of its head. I remember her telling Frau *Tonne that this very gardener, upon being bitten by a poisonous snake, had immediately cut off his hand to stop the venom from spreading. He had then rushed into the house and caused the cook to faint. According to this brave individual, the rounded head of a snake indicates that it is poisonous, the roundness being caused by the poison fangs on each side. The ones with narrow heads are harmless.*

Since the small hospital in Takedao was not equipped to handle any kind of emergency, and certainly not a cut-off hand, Mama did not believe in taking any chances and destroyed any snake that came her way. In fact, her efficient way of dispatching the creatures caused her to be called whenever one was spotted, no matter what time of day. As soon as she heard her name being called from any part of the garden, she would rush to fetch her long iron bar at the back of the house and proceed to the place of the latest sighting.

One evening, an especially large, grayish-black snake was discovered under the boardwalk leading to the dining hall, and, as usual, Mama was immediately called to the scene. The creature was well over a yard long and half of its body, including the head, was out of reach under the walk. Leaving it there posed the danger of its eventually finding its way into the dining room.

After chasing us away to a safe distance, Mama started poking around under the walk with her iron bar, hoping that way to annoy the animal and incite it to slither out from under its partial hiding place. This, however, failed to produce the desired result. Upon checking in the dining room, one older boy reported that the creature appeared to have got its head stuck in a hole in the thin wall of the building, and Mama, iron bar in hand, was able to carry out the execution from that end. She then asked the bigger boys to dispose of the animal as usual, by burying it in the woods and went into the house to wash up and have a much deserved cup of tea.

The minute she was out of sight, however, the boys stopped their trek into the woods and huddled. There was a lot of laughing and snickering, and we little ones crept near to hear what was going on. After chasing us away repeatedly, they finally gave up and swore everyone to secrecy under pain of a thrashing.

The next morning, Mama was wakened at dawn by a lot of giggling and tittering on the veranda overlooking the river.

-Look, here they come! Oh, this is going to be funny!-

-There are four of them! Watch them as they get to the end of the bridge!-

The veranda was teaming with children, including her own, and she just arrived in time to see four nurses tripping across the swinging bridge on their getas. *They were, of course, on their way to work at the hospital, and there was really nothing special about this sight, since they regularly made this trip back and forth from residence to hospital at this hour and several more times during the day. This morning, however, as they neared the end of the bridge, they let out a nerve-tingling shriek and rushed back across the river at top speed, their wooden* getas *clacking loudly. On the other side, they met two of their colleagues just about to cross as well and pointed, still shrieking, to the hotel side of the bridge. Everyone on the veranda, fourteen years and younger, was doubled over with laughter.*

The next thing we saw was Mr. Hendrickson, no doubt wakened by the noise, heading towards the bridge in his pajamas to investigate. He stopped short for a minute, then bent over and with a stick picked up the dead body of yesterday's snake, nicely curled into a pile at a spot on the narrow bridge where the nurses would practically fall over it. He flung it in a neat arc high into the air and towards the river.

*-They thought it was alive! Did you see them run scared?
Oh, that was funny!-*

*Mama, however, was not as amused as we thought she ought
to have been. We tried hard to look guilty, but Baerbel and I
could not stop giggling. That day, during a nature lesson,*
Frau *Tonne told us that it had been a rather dangerous bit of
fun, since the mate of the dead snake often comes in search of
it and might very well have been in the vicinity. But for days
after, we talked of this little adventure with our friends,
imitating the poor, frightened nurses in their headlong flight
across the swinging bridge and making ourselves laugh all
over again.*

*****

It happens quite suddenly in the middle of the night, and so
quickly, that by the time everyone is fully awake and heading
for safety, the water is already up to knee level.

The last two weeks of October have been very wet and cold,
with a steady rain almost every day and the level of the river
unusually high, the water a muddy, gray color. All day long,
the animals around the hotel seemed restless, and Watanabe-
san's dog barked incessantly until *Oma* was ready to throw
her shoe at him. The mule, which was used to bring supplies
to the village, broke loose at suppertime and ran away, and
the pheasants called all evening from the nearby woods. Before
going to bed, Liesel looked out again , but a heavy fog
shrouded the river, so that she could only hear the rushing
water but see nothing.

Towards four in the morning, Else Tonne bangs frantically at Liesel's door. -The river is over the banks, and I think the bridge is already gone! The downstairs is flooded! We have to get out as fast as we can!- She has a candle in her hand because the electricity is out everywhere. -I'll help you dress the children. *Oma* is gathering a few things together.-

Sven comes in with a knapsack on his back, carrying another candle. He volunteers to take the twins up to the little teahouse on the mountain towards which everyone is heading. -Take only your most important things,- he advises. -And hurry! You can take Hannele. Helli and I will come back as soon as possible and tie some of the trunks to the main beam of the house. They might have a chance there. The way the water is rising though, I wouldn't be surprised if the whole place will go.-

It is hard, in a moment of panic to think of what to take. Clothes… warm clothes for the children. Liesel throws everything helter-skelter into a large travelling bag.

-Come, hurry, Liesel!- *Oma* is heading down the stairs. Liesel runs after her, holding Hannele firmly by the hand. The water is a rushing black torrent. She lifts Hannele and slings her bag over her shoulder. Helli is at the door. -Take my hands,- he screams over the rising wind. He is a tall, well-built man, and it is reassuring to feel his strong fingers close around her wrist. He is pulling her, Liesel does not know in what direction, but he has been guiding women and children for the past hour or more, and she trusts herself to him. *Oma* holds on to his other hand. They are wading against the current, in steadily rising water.

B-House, the somewhat smaller other residence, is built on a hill away from the river, but no one is taking a chance. The place is deserted, and everyone is heading up the mountain.

-Most of the children are in the teahouse,- Helli shouts, when they have reached relatively dry land. -Sven has taken the twins and Else up there. Oh, here he comes back now.-

Sven is running down the path. -The twins are with Else,- he tells Liesel. -We have to hurry, if we are going to save anything. It's just light enough to see the river from up there. In fact, all you can see is river. It must be the dam! Look, there's a table from the dining hall! Helli, hop on, we'll get there faster that way.- They laugh as they jump on to the floating table, and, waving jauntily, they disappear into the damp grayness.

Liesel says a silent prayer, as she and *Oma*, with Hannele between them, trudge up the slippery path. The teahouse is divided into two big glassed-in rooms. The luggage, bags, blankets and children, who are jumping on everything, are in one room, and most of the mothers are in the other. Someone is making tea on a hibachi. The noise is unbelievable, but the place is dry and warm.

Liesel immediately begins to worry about the number of people crammed together in this tiny house, perched on the mountainside, which was surely never built for such a crowd. -Let's try to keep the children from jumping too much,- she tells some of the mothers.

-We are far too many people for such a small place, and with all the rain we have had, this could be dangerous.- They decide to divide the weight of people and luggage as evenly as possible between the two rooms, and then take turns entertaining the children with stories and word games to keep them quiet.

In the gray light of dawn, the buildings below become more clearly visible.

-There's Uncle Helli!- Hannele cries. They watch Helli and one of the other marines dangling from the rafters of A-House, as they try to throw a number of ropes over the main beam. Having finally succeeded, they lower the ends of the ropes to someone below, and up swings a huge net, holding odd trunks and bags, in fact, just about everything they could lay their hands on in the still dry upper rooms. -There's our blue trunk, Mami,- Hannele cries again. The children are fascinated by the maneuvers below.

A short time later, a thoroughly wet band of marines and Sven arrive at the tea house.

-We've done all we can for the time being.- Sven reports. -Let's hope the main structure holds.- He looks around at the confusion in the little teahouse and frowns. - The men feel that B-House is up high enough, even if the river rises several more feet. I think some of us should think of going down there. This place could give way under our weight.-

The families with older children are soon moved, while the luggage and the mothers with smaller children stay in the teahouse for the time being. This means that less than half the former crowd remains in the little mountain place, and Liesel and the girls spend much of the time at the large windows watching the scene below.

-Mami, look! A house!- Baerbel and Resel point to the river below and, sure enough, the little white house from about a mile up the road, a fairly strong structure, by Japanese standards, is drifting down the gray, swirling waters at top speed. Next, they break out in giggles as they watch an old dressing table from one of the bedrooms, with the washbasin still on it, sail around the corner of A-House. They have been up since four o'clock and are worn out, and soon they are laughing and crying at the same time. Liesel takes them away from the windows and arranges some makeshift beds with bags and blankets, but it is quite impossible to make them settle down.

Hours crawl by. The scene below is a mass of water and debris. Liesel's eyes are riveted to the main beam of A-House. It is still holding, but badly curving. Any minute now it could give way, and all her worldly possessions would be drifting down the raging mountain stream. -But we are safe,- she keeps telling herself. -We are safe, and we could have been drowned.- She wonders if the Japanese villagers have made it out in time. Of Watanabe-*san* and his family there has been no sign. Despite their differences in the past, she likes the man and worries what might have happened to him.

At last, she sees Sven toiling his way up the hill again. He slips several times on the slushy ground. -I think it is safe to come down now,- he announces. -I'd really rather see you there than here. This little bird's nest increasingly gives me the chills when I look up from down there.-

As they trudge down hill with as much luggage as they can carry, he tells Liesel that she and the children will have to share a six-*tatami* room with *Oma* Becker and Else. -I'm afraid it will be crowded,- he grins. -You know that B-House is the smaller of the two houses, and now we're all there together. But it's a nice little room and somewhat by itself, downstairs, in a corner of the house. The fellows and I have tried to divide the available space as evenly as possible. We'll share a room between the six of us. A *tatami* each,- he laughs.

B-House is still completely dry, and the river has not risen any higher in the past hour. The place is, of course, teeming with people. Liesel wonders wearily why some people always have to shout to carry on a conversation.

-The kitchen building is still relatively dry.- Helli tells them. -The fellows and I are going over there to see about some food. I'm afraid it's going to be strict rationing all over again. The storage shed has gone to the deep.-

-I'm hungry, Mami!- Baerbel wails immediately.

-We'll go to our room and get dry and cozy first, and then Mami will see about some bread and tea, okay?- Liesel pats Baerbel's shoulder and pushes her gently out of the crowded hall towards their little corner room. *Oma* is there and Else. They have found some blankets and made up a bed for the children. There is a hibachi in the corner by the windows, and Else has hot tea ready.

162

Everyone has a cup, and then the children, warm and dry now, forget about food and fall asleep almost before Liesel has tucked them in.

***

It was the dam. Unable to hold out against the rain-swollen river, it caved in and caused the flood. For miles, the countryside is in ruins. Only B-House and the hospital, which, because of their location on a raised level of land were never really threatened, are still standing. The nurses who were on duty the night of the flood have moved into the hospital with the few patients who have been there throughout most of the war.

For a week now, the river has been receding, and several days of dry weather have caused the earth to harden, so that walking along the former road, which is now not much more than a narrow track, is now relatively safe. The Japanese villagers are slowly returning from the mountains, where they had fled the evening of the disaster. They are finding their village in total ruin, with almost all the houses completely washed away by the river. Many of them are preparing to hike over the mountains to Kobe to stay with relatives. The Watanabes are back also and have moved into the teahouse.

The frame of A-House is still standing. The men have lowered the net, and Liesel has most of her belongings. But there are so many small things missing. The children's dolls, Willi's framed picture, and her diamond ring. She always takes it off at night, and now, of course, it is gone.

-I can see why you are upset. It would certainly be an expensive loss,- one of the women says, when Liesel first notices that it is not on her finger. But Liesel does not really care about the monetary value of her ring. -It is his face when he gave it to me, his kiss when he held me tight. It is a hundred memories and a feeling of closeness and belonging when I see it on my finger and touch it… ,- she thinks sadly.

The women search the rubble of A-House every day, hoping to find some of the lost items. -There is doll number three!- Else cries. She pulls at the red skirt of Baerbel's cloth doll and holds it up. -That's all of them now. A good wash, and they'll be as good as new.- They are making their way out of the mess of stone, mud, and fallen beams. Liesel smiles happily. Yesterday, she found Willi's picture in its broken frame, and today, the last of the dolls. Her three little mothers will be glad.

Suddenly, they hear a shout. A plane is slowly circling over the area as if searching for something, and people are down by the river waving frantically. The pilot tips his wings and takes off again.

-He couldn't possibly land,- Helli says, shaking his head. -But at least we know now that they are aware of the situation. Watanabe-*san* promised that the villagers would report the disaster to the authorities.-

-He's coming back!- someone shouts excitedly. -Look, he is going to fly right over us! He wants to throw something! Watch out! They are going to throw down provisions!-

The little hatch at the side of the plane opens, and a bundle is hurled out. The group of onlookers watches with fascination as it tumbles towards the ground and then, with horror, as the package is swayed by a strong gust of wind and, missing the narrow space of land between the river and the mountain, is carried away by the strong current of the stream.

-Oh, Lord! Our food! Oh, what are they going to do now?-

The plane circles and tries again. Another bundle, another miss. The pilot flies on, and the group on the ground feels utterly dejected. And then, there he is again, coming back from the other direction.

-Smart fellow!- Helli cries. -This way he has more room to maneuver. Look there! He is right over the house now!-

The bundle is hurled from the other side of the plane and lands safely on the rocks not far from B-House. -Look out! Another one! Here it comes!- Everyone is laughing with excitement, as the marines carry the packets to the small yard in front of the house, and the plane, once again tipping its wings, takes off, this time for good.

-Peanut butter! Look at the cans of peanut butter!-

-Biscuits and cans of beans! Chocolate! Look, we have chocolate! And canned milk! Thank God for that!-

-There is a letter too!- Sven rips open the waterproof envelope. -It appears that rescue operations are underway!- he smiles. –

They say that the highway on our side of the river is completely washed out, and a crossing of the river has to be attempted. The only bridge left for miles around is the one that brings the drinking water from across the river. The one about half a mile from here. That's accessible from our side only via the cliffs. The American troops will try to cross over to us and assist in evacuating the children. They suggest that the adults will have to circumvent the cliff with the aid of ropes and then to crawl across on the water pipes. They are asking us to take only necessary items and to be ready by noon the day after tomorrow. Other valuables will be sent after us when the situation has improved.-

The next few days are frantic with preparations. Winter is coming, and everyone will need warm clothes. That is the most important thing. Liesel packs a knapsack for each of the girls and herself. They can wear that on their backs and still have their hands free. The knapsacks are makeshift, made from pillowcases, but they serve the purpose.

-Mami, our dolls, We can't leave them now, when we've just got them back again. They can't stay here. They will be lonely!-

-And the teddies, Mami, the teddies too!-

A compromise is reached. The teddies will manage quite well on their own. They are stronger and can stay and look after the rest of the things. But the dolls are stuffed into the knapsacks the very last, so that their heads peek out on top and they will be able to see everything.

***

The evening before the rescue operation is scheduled to start, Liesel searches the rubble one more time. It would take a small miracle to find her ring, she knows. She prays fervently to Saint Anthony, who has helped her find a few things in the past. Gretchen Mueller comes down to help search. She is a lovely looking girl of eighteen and finds Liesel's attachment to her ring very romantic. While they look, she chats away and tells Liesel how much she likes Helli.

-He thinks because of his burns no one could care for him anymore,- she says. - But I think he is so brave and well..., so sensitive, you know? He was so kind to me during the flood and didn't think it stupid when I was scared and started to cry.- She stands up straight for a minute to ease her back and looks at Liesel with a sidelong, shy glance.

-You know, he..., well... , he actually kissed me then. Oh, just a quick kiss. I'm sure it didn't mean anything to him. He is a marine after all, and he must have kissed lots of girls before. But it was nice.-

-Why do you think he did not mean anything by it?- Liesel asks. -Helli doesn't strike me as someone who simply kisses any girl that comes along.-

-Well, he hasn't talked to me since,- she blurts out, suddenly upset. -He actually avoids me now. He probably felt sorry for me, that's all.-

-Maybe he avoids you because he is shy. As you say, he worries about the burns on his face so much. He may be afraid of what you think of him.- Liesel knows that she is an incurable romantic. But somehow, Gretchen and Helli seem just right for each other.

Suddenly Gretchen gasps. -*Frau* Fiand! Oh *Frau* Fiand! I think I found it!- Her eyes are huge with surprise. -Your ring, *Frau* Fiand, here is your ring! I am sure it is! I saw something glitter as the sun hit it just now. Just at the right moment when I happened to be looking, and the sun was just at the right angle. See, it is setting, and in a minute it will be gone behind the mountains. Oh, *Frau* Fiand, I'm so glad for you!- She hold out the diamond ring. Her hands are trembling. Liesel puts her arms around the girl and hugs her. She is literally speechless. She had never truly believed that she would ever see it again, and here it is, glimmering in the evening light. Gretchen puts it on Liesel's finger, and the two women stand there for a moment lost for words.

They go back to the little room in B-House. In her knapsack Liesel has a small case that had been stored away in the blue trunk, a few things she had picked up in Kyoto before the bombing blocked out all other thoughts. Liesel picks out a lovely pearl broach and pins it on Gretchen's dress. -Think of me when you wear this,- she tells her with a smile. And remember that miracles do still happen from time to time. You will never know how much this means to me.-

That evening, Liesel, Else and *Oma* have a farewell celebration in their little room. Sven is there and Helli, and Liesel invites Gretchen to come. Call it matchmaking, but then, why not? When they leave, Helli walks Gretchen to her family's room, and they are holding hands.

***

The American Army, right on schedule, starts arriving around noon the following morning. Liesel's English is limited, and it seems to her that they all speak as though they have hot potatoes in their mouths, but she can make out the general drift of what is being said.

The children will be handed up the steep side of the cliff from hand to hand. G.I.s will be stationed on every small crevice in the rock, and they will hand the children upwards to the top, where another G.I. will take them piggyback across the wooden planks that have been laid over the water pipes. All other residents, fourteen and over, will be required to swing by their hands along a rope leading around the cliff to the other, more easily climbable side and then make their way up the cliff and across the pipes. There will be plenty of men handy to shout encouragements and assist in every way possible, but it will be up to all persons to do their individual best.

Liesel thinks that maybe it does not seem too difficult to these men to swing by their hands from a rope over a precipice, with an angry mountain stream gurgling below. Probably nothing would seem impossible to them after some of the action they have been through, but she looks at *Oma* and shudders.

The children are lined up in a row. She kisses the girls as each bravely takes the big hand of a strange man in khaki. The G.I.s grin when they see the dolls, and one of them turns to Liesel before leading Resel off towards the cliff. -They'll be all right, Ma'am,- he says, smiling. -Don't you worry none.

They'll be waiting for you on the other side.- He smacks his gum, and then, remembering, reaches into his shirt pocket and gives Resel a stick of gum. He offers one to Liesel as well. -Helps the nerves,- he grins, winking at her, and takes off, with Resel marching and chewing confidently at his side, telling him all about her teddy that had to stay behind and look after things. She seems oblivious of the fact that he probably doesn't understand a word of German.

Liesel waits until she sees the girls safely lifted up the rock. Once up there, they wave down to her, and she decides to try her luck at getting across. *Oma* is at her side. Helli offers to go directly in front of *Oma* and Sven behind, then Else, Liesel, and Miriam Faust. It is a slow, painful process. Liesel's arms ache, and she worries about *Oma*.

-You're doing just fine, just fine. Just a little more now. Don't look down.- The G.I.s call out calmly and reassuringly, and Sven speaks quietly to *Oma*. Liesel looks to her right at Miriam Faust, who toils along beside her, her long body swaying slowly from side to side, and she suddenly has a mental picture of what they must all look like and wants to laugh. God knows it isn't funny, but it takes a superhuman effort to control herself, and when they reach the ground again, on the other side of the cliff, she breaks down into sobs of laughter.

Someone pats her on the shoulder. -It's all right now, lady. It's all right. No sweat the rest of the way.- A G.I. with a huge mustache is kneeling in front of her as she sits on the gravel laughing, with tears running down her face. The others are standing around her with pained expressions on their faces, and suddenly it isn't funny anymore. She shakes her head and wipes her eyes. -I'm sorry. I don't know what got into me.-

The children, safely on the other side by now, watch as she crawls across the pipes, and then they are in her arms, and everything is fine again. -Thank God, that is over!-

XV

*O*ver the past years, whenever I have read or heard negative reports involving American G.I.s in military theatres, such as Vietnam, Panama, Somalia or elsewhere, I have found it difficult to reconcile these accounts with my happier memories of post-war Japan.

For most of us war-weary refugees, far from home, hungry and frightened, the American soldiers were hero figures. We children saw them as an endless source of chewing gum, Butterfinger chocolate bars, piggy-back rides and the occasional ride in a big green jeep. For Hannele, they represented her first childhood love. They were reassuring, friendly and unfailingly kind. And they saw us, I believe, as a little bit of home.

Hidden, underneath cartons of shirts to be mended, which they brought to Mama every week, there were packets of butter, peanuts, sugar, and other goods. They introduced us to the funnies, which, although we could not understand them, provided hours of entertainment, while we made up our own stories to go along with the pictures. Baerbel and I were nicknamed the Katzenjammer Kids, and 'Uncle' Dick and 'Uncle' Jack took us fishing and sailing on Lake Hakone.

Mama became the sounding board for all their troubles, their replacement older sister, mother, friend. They came on Christmas Eve and hummed along with the familiar carols as best they could, played checkers with us and laughed.

And somehow those memories will stay with me forever, come what may, in this world of more sophisticated weaponry and psychological brainwashing of troops before combat. For me, the American G.I. will always have a bit of a halo around his head, because as a small child, I found comfort in his big hand that held mine and his shoulders that carried me across a wild mountain stream.

*****

The American Army barracks at Takaratzka are an ugly group of gray, one story buildings, each marked with huge, black numbers that are painted right onto the gray tarpaper-like siding. There are two main entrances to each building, one on each end of the long, rectangular structures. A dark corridor, lined with countless doors, connects the two.

Liesel's group is among the first to arrive. A sergeant opens the tarpaulin flaps on the army truck that has brought them so far and then starts to call out names, checking them off as people jump off the truck. It is the same list that they made during boarding, and it would seem that they are making sure everyone is still there. How anyone could have jumped off a truck that was completely roped in by tarpaulin and going sixty miles an hour is hard to imagine, let alone why such an attempt would have been made. But then, organization and red tape go hand in hand, and Liesel is getting her first taste of endless lists and waiting lines.

A dismal, fine rain is falling and, by the time they are finally marched off towards one of the buildings, they are all uncomfortably moist and cold. *Oma* is with Liesel, looking tired, worried and old. Miriam Faust is also with this first group, but Helli, Sven and Else have stayed behind to help board the other women with children and will probably be on the last truck.

They are directed to a large room in No.8 barracks. Bunk beds line the walls. The room sleeps ten. Liesel's heart sinks when she sees the dreary green walls, the gray iron beds and the one table in the middle of the room under a bare light bulb. What a dreadful place! She has a strong urge to sit down and cry. It has all been just a bit too much. But then, as usual, common sense sets in. -You have just been saved from a crowded, hungry winter in a forsaken mountain village. Be grateful for what you have,- she tells herself sternly. -And we'll stay here not a minute longer than absolutely necessary!- she adds.

With what she hopes is a bright smile and a cheery voice, she cries. -Well, look at the nice warm room and all those clean beds!- Hannele and the twins watch her suspiciously. Whenever, in all their travels they have had to stop a while, Liesel has always somehow managed to make a cozy, little nest for her family. But this 'hall,' with the smell of antiseptic pervading the air, is not convertible into anything home-like, and the girls know it.

The Fausts are crowding in behind Liesel and the girls. With *Oma*, that makes nine. Franz and Joseph immediately climb into two of the top bunks and start jumping around, yodeling with delight. Quick action is needed if sanity is to be saved. -Come girls, we'll take the beds on this side,- Liesel says, keeping up her forced cheerfulness. -We'll put our knapsacks on this ledge here and you can get into some dry clothes.-

-How are we going to do that?- Hannele whispers. -Gert and Franz and Joseph are going to look.-

-No, no,- Miriam Faust interjects immediately. -The boys will change in the washrooms across the corridor.- That solves one problem, at least for the time being.

Once everyone is dry, the moist clothes are hung over the railings at the end of each bed. -Tomorrow things will look better.- Liesel tells herself. She will find some clotheslines and a wash kitchen. There must surely be a lounge somewhere as well, and a place for the children to play.

Trucks keep rolling up, and, through the dingy windows, they watch as more and more families alight and are ushered towards their building. -I think most of us will be in No.8,- *Oma* says. The girls keep looking for their friends and shout with excitement every time they spot a familiar face. Towards seven o'clock, a shrill bell sounds. Feet can be heard outside. -Dinner, everyone! This way please!- a man's voice shouts. They put on their still wet coats and follow the crowd across the yard towards a brightly lit hall.

-Well, there you are!- Sven Hendrickson is at Liesel's elbow. - You're in No.8 aren't you? Else, Helli and I are in No.6. The last arrivals were put in there. Dismal looking place, isn't it?-

Else comes running up to them, and Helli waves from further up the line. Suddenly Liesel feels a lot better. After all, she has friends, and they are not far away.

-I hear there is a pile of mail for us here,- Sven says. -We'll probably get it tomorrow.-

Six months have gone by since the last letter from Willi. Only a few words had been inked out, and Liesel hopes that now, with the war over, they won't censor the letters so strictly. Surely there will be a letter from him, maybe even two. He had written that Wilma's husband, Hans Reis, was dying of cancer. -I am with him daily. He knows that he will never see his homeland again, and this causes him the greatest anguish, I think. That, and the thought that he will have no one to carry on his name. How lucky we are, you and I, in our girls, in our health, and in our love.- Maybe there will be a letter tomorrow. Things are looking better all the time.

Everyone takes a huge tin tray that is divided into differently shaped sections. The food is plopped onto the tray, into the various divisions, and thus, when one is finished, one returns only one dirty dish to be washed in the steaming gray dish machine behind the cooks. Tonight, there are mashed potatoes, baked ham, peas and creamed corn. What a feast! The girls watch with round eyes as the tall black cook is filling their tray. They have never seen a black person before and are frankly amazed, but, thank God, they remember to keep quiet for once. The cook winks at them and scoops up an extra helping of pudding for each of them. Once seated, Liesel explains to them that there are many black Americans, and that they are simply a different race, just as they themselves are different from the Japanese, and that people do not like to be stared at. The girls don't quite believe her, since they received an extra portion of pudding from the nice black man.

Sven says that No.6 barracks has a recreation hall as well as a small lounge, which will be made available to the refugees, and he promises to find out about laundry facilities. No one stays long over dinner. The hall is bright and noisy, and everyone is tired out. It has been an eventful day.

The next morning, Hannele and the twins run out to play in the large, gray yard, while Liesel lingers over her second cup of real, honest-to-goodness coffee. The morning is bright and sunny, though with a distinct chill in the air. Winter is coming.

When she leaves the dining hall, she sees a tall white-haired officer bending down in front of Hannele, his hands on his knees. He is trying to draw her into a conversation and is smiling and nodding at her. She stares at him with a puzzled frown and then, suddenly, smiling brightly, starts jabbering in Japanese. He pulls a face and shakes his head. Straightening up, he sees Liesel watching and asks, -Your little girl?- When she nods, he smiles. -She speaks Japanese well,- he says with admiration and reaches out to stroke Hannele's curly head. Then, nodding briefly in Liesel's direction, he walks towards the office buildings, where several men salute him as he enters.

The letters are handed out at noon in the dining hall. There is only one for Liesel from Sister Olga in Saginomia. Liesel finds it hard to swallow her disappointment. Nothing from Willi!

- My dearest Liesel,

I am sending this in the hope that it will reach you safe and sound. We have heard of the terrible flood in Takedao and, consequently, I have not dared send on any of your other mail in case it might be lost. There are several letters here from Dehra Dun. With the war now over, they seem to have lifted the restrictions somewhat, but some of your husband's letters look as though they may have been written some time ago and traveled extensively.

We hear that you will be quartered in army barracks until other accommodations can be found for you. I am writing to say that, thanks to the dear Lord, Olga House is still standing, and your two rooms here are still vacant. They have sent me a varied selection of German, Italian and Hungarian boarders. Frau Sacca is back, as I predicted. The others are all strangers. I would be so happy if you could come back, but I don't know how long I can hold your rooms for you. Oma Becker is, of course, welcome, but she would have to share your rooms.

Do let me know as soon as possible. The food situation is manageable, now that the war is over. Hoping to hear from you shortly.

Your loving friend,   Olga -

-Here is my ticket out of this place!- Liesel thinks jubilantly. -Two nice rooms for the children, *Oma* and me! A garden to play in for the girls! I will go to see the officer in charge right away and, meanwhile, send a message to Olga to hold those rooms for me, as well as my letters. She writes that there are several of them!-

***

Already more than a week has gone by! The forms to fill out, the questions to answer! There seems to be no end in sight! The Americans seem content to keep everyone in Takaratzka! Only those with definite destinations are even considered for permission to leave, and that permission has to be obtained from the commander in charge, personally. To see this gentleman, one has to have an appointment and, even then, one is not at all sure of getting into the big man's office. Liesel has waited in lines and waiting rooms every day for over a week now, and she is about ready to give up.

Sister Olga will not be able to hold her rooms indefinitely. If this goes on much longer, they will have to be turned over to others. Each day, while she stands in line, usually in a drafty corridor outside some office or other, *Oma* watches the children. She is as anxious as Liesel to move back to Saginomia. The room in No.8 barrack, which seemed so big and bare the night of their arrival, has become oppressively confining. The children are fighting constantly. They have not been able to go out to run off their pent-up energy because the weather has been so cold, with rain or sleet almost every day since their arrival. Miriam Faust, instead of helping to settle disputes, sits and sulks when anyone speaks sharply to her children. There is no place to hang clothes outside, and the wash lines that have been strung along the ceiling of their room are almost always full. The luggage from Takedao has not arrived as yet, and they have only one change of clothing. Franz still wets his bed, and, on rainy days, the place smells damp and musty.

-Look, here he comes! That's the commander in charge!- Someone whispers to Liesel, as a tall white-haired man, whom she immediately recognizes as the officer who spoke to Hannele the morning after their arrival, comes walking down the hall. He is in the middle of saying something to the officer beside him, when he sees Liesel looking at him, and he stops abruptly. For a moment, he seems to be trying to remember, and then, suddenly, he smiles and nods, before disappearing through the door, which a saluting G.I. is holding open for him.

-Do you know him?- Several people ask surprised.

-No, no, of course not.- Liesel feels her face flush. -I only saw him outside one morning when he was talking to the children.-

The wait goes on. The line begins to move, then stops. Time drags on. Liesel knows that she won't make it to the door again today. How long is this going to go on? At five, the office closes. Weary and thoroughly depressed, she heads towards the outside stairs, when she suddenly hears a voice behind her.

-Madam? Madam! Wait a moment, please!- She turns to see a young officer running after her. -The Major will see you now, if you'd care to come with me, please.-

She stares at him in surprise. He grins and shrugs. -The Major said he wanted to see the little lady with the brown hair in a roll around her head. That's you, I think. Said to bring you in, even if you didn't make it to the door.- He frowns and shakes his head.

- Been a pretty long wait again today, hasn't it? Sorry we can't seem to speed things up.-

-Yes.- Liesel can't think of what else to say. She doesn't speak English very well and feels totally puzzled. The commander gets up as she enters. He stretches out a big brown hand and smiles. -We met about a week ago, if I remember correctly. My name is MacDonald, Bob MacDonald.-

-I am Liesel Fiand…, *Frau* Liesel Fiand,- she stammers. - Excuse me, please, but my English…. . I speak not so good.-

-That's quite all right. Like my Japanese, I suppose,- he laughs. -Now your little daughter, the one with the cute pigtails, she has no problem with languages. Chatters away in Japanese, just like a native. I imagine she would learn English pretty quickly too.-

-Oh, Hannele! *Ja*, she is now already at English to learn,- Liesel smiles, somewhat reassured by his friendly voice.

- Ha-nne-le,- he pronounces the name carefully. -I have a granddaughter who has long, curly hair like Ha-nne-le. She wears it in pigtails too, with pink ribbons. She would be about ten now. Your little Ha-nne-le reminds me very much of my granddaughter. But I have not seen her now for three years.- He smiles ruefully. -Time goes by so quickly. She probably wouldn't even know me now.-

Liesel is not quite sure what to say. He is looking at her, but she knows that he is thinking of home and family. A man of authority and power, no doubt envied by many, but just now, he would probably rather be at home. -My Hannele will eight be in May,- she says quietly.

-Yes,- he says. -Mary was eight the spring after I went overseas.- He smiles. - She wanted a pony then. A horse of her own. My wife writes that she is a very good rider now.- He pulls out a picture from his wallet and shows Liesel a little girl in pigtails, smiling brightly astride a shaggy pony.

-Hannele had also a pony, before the war, in Sarangan. But she was still very much too little,- Liesel hears herself say, and then she feels suddenly awkward at having mentioned the war. They were getting along so well, but now she feels herself blush, as she gives him back his picture.

-You had wanted to see me about something, Mrs. Fiand? - he reminds her quietly.

-Yes, Major MacDonald.- She has learned this little speech by heart with the help of Sven and speaks very quickly now. -

I have an opportunity to take the children to Saginomia, near Tokyo, where we lived before our evacuation to Takedao. A friend has rooms for us there in a home that has been approved by the authorities. There is a garden for the children. We would have a little more room and some privacy. It is not that I don't feel grateful for all that has been done for us here, but... , well, it would be better... , I think. ... And there is a garden where they can play... and everything... .-

He looks at her application in front of him. -You have three little girls?- He asks, looking at her with interest. -*Ja*.- Liesel smiles and produces a picture of the twins and Hannele, taken in Takedao.

He nods. -Identical twins,- he says, and then he frowns. -You did not have much to eat there, I think.-

Liesel turns quite red. She had not even realized how emaciated the children looked. She takes the picture and puts it in her purse, and looks at him without saying a word.

-I will check out this Olga House,- he promises. -I'll do my best for you, Mrs. Fiand. I understand how you feel.- He smiles.

Liesel suddenly remembers *Oma*. -Major, please, there is too an elderly *Frau* . She was with me during the..., *na*, since we to Japan came. She needs really someone, and ... I am hoping... . There is also place for her in the Olga House. I will my rooms gladly with her share ... .-

He seems surprised and looks at Liesel curiously, and then, with what she fears is a certain brusqueness, he asks for *Oma*'s full name and history. For a minute she feels that perhaps she has asked for too much and that he is now annoyed with her. But what could she have done? She could not have left *Oma* behind after all they had been through. She had had no choice but to ask for her leave permit as well.

He sees her anxious expression and, rising, he holds out his hand again, smiling now.

-Mrs. Fiand, you have three beautiful daughters,- he says. -But they also have a beautiful mother. You are a kind and generous woman. Your permits and Mrs. Becker's will be ready tomorrow. Good-bye, Mrs. Fiand, and God bless you.-

XVI

<u>*Eight letters from Willi*</u>

<u>*Atjeh, Sumatra, August 1940 –*</u>

Mein Herzele,

I can feel your anguish like a physical pain. Never was I more certain of the close ties that bind our hearts and minds. All this is a heavy burden for your small shoulders to carry, mein Liesele. *If only I could help you in some way! I am with you constantly in my thoughts and dreams!*

<u>*January 1941*</u>

Always I am wondering about you and our three little flowers; how they must be blossoming forth; in what circumstances you find yourselves now. I go back into the past and feel you in my arms again. But I cannot do this often. We must remain strong. If only I could receive a word from you! To know you are well.

September 1941

Today I received a telegram from you. I also have the pictures you sent through a Colonel VanDecker. You have lost so much weight, mein Liesele. *Do stay well for me,* mein Herz. *The little ones are so adorable!*

Dehra Dun, British India, 1942

We have now arrived in our permanent detention quarters here in British India. They are the best we have had so far. The climate is good, the area beautiful, and our barracks are roomy and clean. We have enough to eat.

Since our arrival here, I have been assigned regular kitchen duties. I am always healthy and try to do my best for my five hundred comrades. They seem to be very satisfied with my services and have appointed me official 'chief of the stomach brigade.' I have a large working area and like being busy.

October 1944

I try so hard to imagine how big the girls are now. Sometimes I am shocked at the thought that the little ones are already four years old and Hannele six. Often I look at children's pictures in the magazines we occasionally get from home, and I try to imagine that maybe the girls look like this or that child now. I get mail from Germany on a fairly regular basis. If only I would receive word from you!

I Cry For Innocence

Hans Reis is not well. I am worried about him and suspect the worst.

My thoughts are always the same. My belief in our Heimatland *and in the future is undaunted. Courage, and love for the paths of home are the pillars of being. Through unending past generations and as a bridge to endless rows of future men and women we two have become one and have given the best within us to our children for the future, that they might carry it within them and pass it on in time to come. I know that you cherish and protect this within them. Give them much love, Liesele, also from their father, and tell them about me. Let us direct our thoughts to the future,* mein Herz, *when we will once again be united and together will build a new life for ourselves.*

April 1945

I will never forget the last three months. Hans died as courageously as he lived. I spent all my waking hours at his bedside. Please assure Wilma and Oma *of his love till the very end. I have written to them but have not heard from them. I am so worried for their sake.*

August 1945

I saw a picture today, in a magazine. Two people are walking through the beautiful hills and meadows of home. Maybe soon now we will be together there!

Now that this war is finally over, many are talking of going back to the Dutch Indies, but I do not believe that there is anything left for us there anymore. We must go home to Germany, mein Schatz. *It would not be right not to do our part in trying to rebuild our dear homeland. At least let us try to do what we can, when we can.*

I believe firmly and with confidence that, despite our many years of separation, we will understand each other even better and become even closer to one another, just as we did after our wedding day. Even if today the world seems to be standing on its head as far as marriage and loyalty are concerned, and one hears so many incredible stories, we two will remain old fashioned in that respect, won't we?

Do give the children my dearest love. I am so looking forward to seeing them and pray daily for an early reunion. I yearn for you mein liebstes Herzele.

Immer,
Dein Willimann

*****

Saginomia has not changed. Olga House still stands, surrounded by its large, shady trees. The airfield and several neighboring houses have been destroyed, but otherwise, all is the same. Liesel is glad to be back. Children need a home-like atmosphere with a regular routine. The last few weeks have been chaotic for everyone, and she is anxious to settle down for a while, but it was hard to say good-bye to her Takedao friends.

-I would not go back there for anything,- Else told her, when she heard that Liesel had leave permits for herself and *Oma*. -But then, you could always manage Sister Olga.- She and Sven are planning to find Karl in Hakone as soon as possible, and Sven hopes to work for the American occupation force after that.

Helli did not know his destination yet, but he is planning to stay close to Gretchen. Liesel feels as though she has lost her family. They have been through so much together, and, although everyone promised to stay in touch, she knows by now how these things work out, and she feels bereft and lonely.

Willi's letters do much to improve her morale. -He is well and he loves me!- she tells herself over and over again. -After all these months without news from him, how I needed these worlds of reassurance! I only realize it now. I must try not to think too much, because thinking leads to wondering, and I have to stay strong! He loves me still, and he feels as I do that we are still one!-

Liesel now shares the smaller bedroom with the children at night, and *Oma* uses the day bed in the sitting room. It is a bit crowded, but Sister Olga has promised that *Oma* can have the next room that becomes vacant. *Frau* Sacca is in her old room, on the second floor. Across from her, in Else's former room, lives Aida Weissmueller, an Italian widow. Her German husband, with whom she had come to Japan on a business holiday, had died of a heart attack a week after the war broke out, leaving her stranded in Japan.

Liesel finds all this out the first time she meets this tall, statuesque and somewhat boisterous lady, about an hour after their arrival in Olga House, when she finds *Signora* Weissmueller at her door with a box of candy for the children, a truly amazing gift in war-torn Japan.

Aida Weissmueller is the type of person who is either in second heaven or in deepest hell. Thank God it is usually the former. An endless chatterer, she confides to Liesel that her 'dear Otto' had been older than she by about twenty years and that, when they had traveled together, he would invariably be taken for her father. Even today she still thinks this hilariously funny and mimics how furious he used to be at such a mistake. She says that after her husband died, she almost committed suicide, and then she rushes on to state that she has a weight problem because, when they were first married, she had a craving for eggs and used to consume close to two dozen a day.

In her room, she has a large urn which, as she tells the children, contains 'her dear Otto' from whom she cannot bear to be parted. The first Liesel hears of this is when Baerbel tells her in a whisper that *Tante* Aida's Otto lives in a large vase with a lid on it, and then looks at Liesel with big, questioning eyes, expecting her to explain this strange situation.

Aida has a vast variety of Italian friends to whom Liesel is constantly being introduced. At gatherings, Aida is without fail the center of attention. One cannot help but like her.

Several days after Liesel's return to Saginomia, Aida tells her that she is very worried about Heinz Mann. When Liesel looks puzzled, she explains , -You know, that man they arrested here in Tokyo about two years ago, right during the worst of the war. That tall, blond business man. Good looking. He had some connection with America at one time or another, an export business of some sort. You must know him! They thought he might be a spy or something like that.-

Liesel vaguely recalls a tall North German man by that name. She had met him once at a gathering in the German House in Tokyo. Kaete Zimmermann had introduced them. She remembers that he had a good sense of humor and an easy laugh. They had had a lot of fun that evening, but when she thinks back now, she remembers feeling surprised that none of their other acquaintances had joined them at their table. -Why are you worried about him?- she now asks Aida. -Is he sick?-

-Why, he is right here!- she exclaims. -And I think he is very ill. When the Americans took over, they let him out of prison, but he had no place to go, and he was very weak. He walked around Tokyo in a sort of daze, I guess, and when he could not walk any more, he simply sat down on the curb. It must have been near his former home, because his old Japanese housemaid found him crawling along the sidewalk. She hardly recognized him. He has a long red beard now, and he is very, very thin!

-The maid helped him to her house and then brought him here in a rickshaw. He is downstairs in that little room under the stairs, but no one really cares what happens to him. Once in a while, he gets up to come to dinner, but he looks just awful! And I think

191

that Sister Olga does not want him here. But I suppose she could not refuse to let him in, since the old maid had hired a rickshaw to bring him all the way out here.-

-That little room beneath the stairs again!- Liesel thinks of Frau Wesel. -Is that where all the unwelcome guests end up?-

The next morning after breakfast, she confronts Sister about Heinz Mann. -Why, I did not know he was staying here! - she exclaims, as though he were a long lost friend. -It will be so nice to see him again! Which room is his?-

-Oh, Liesel! Do you really know him?- Sister moans, dropping her voice to a whisper, even though they are quite alone. -I am sure you do not realize the embarrassment his being here causes me! He worked for the enemy during the war, you know. And now that he is here, people will no doubt think that I condone this sort of thing. Thank God, he does not come out of his room very often. I shudder every time I see him!-

-How do you know that he worked for the 'enemy,' Olga? - Liesel asks her. -Was he ever proven guilty?-

-Why he was imprisoned, wasn't he? Isn't that enough?- Sister is immediately on the defensive. -They wouldn't simply put a man away for no reason at all, would they?...- Her confidence fades when she sees Liesel's face.

-Plenty of innocent people are imprisoned during war time, Olga. Some are still there.- Liesel tells her quietly. She is so angry, that she can hardly keep her voice steady. -At any rate, now that the worst is over, the sooner we learn to live together again, the better for all concerned. I'd like to see him, if you don't mind. I have a feeling he would like to see a friend.-

Liesel knocks on the door several times before she hears a muffled sound that vaguely resembles 'Come in!'. He is in bed, covered up to the chin with a dirty blanket and shaking like a leaf. His eyes have a glassy, feverish look and, of course, he does not recognize her. In the corner of his room is a pile of dirty linen, clothes are strewn all over the floor, and a tray of untouched food on his bedside table gives a sour smell to the room.

-I'm so cold.- He can barely bring out the words. His teeth are chattering. Liesel fetches more blankets from her room and piles them on him. She hopes this is only a minor attack. Willi used to have bouts of *Schuettelfrost* every now and then, a left-over from a tropical infection he had caught years ago. This looks like the same thing, but she will get in touch with Doctor Sato as soon as she can. He was always so kind when the girls were sick, she is sure he will help now.

She dares not open the window, but, once the smelly tray is removed, she gathers up the dirty linen and takes it out to the wash kitchen. Sister Olga and the maids are conspicuously out of sight, but the kindling in the wood stove is easily lit, and while she is putting his underclothes and sheets into the boiler, the old cook, who knows her from pre-Takedao days, waddles out to the wash kitchen and tells her she will finish the job for her.

Liesel picks up a pail and scrub-brush from the kitchen and goes back to her patient's room. He is still shaking so that the bed rattles. She decides to start by scrubbing the room with disinfectant soap for the time being and to wait with the much needed airing until he is fully awake and feeling better. She is so intent on her work, that she is completely startled when she looks up and sees him watching her with curious, but now almost completely clear eyes. He has stopped shaking and lies quietly, bathed in perspiration. -It will be over soon now,- he whispers. -Who are you?-

-I am an old friend of yours,- she smiles. -Liesel Fiand. We met at the German House during the war. Kaete Zimmermann introduced us. I'd like to shake your hand, but, I'm afraid mine are wet and dirty, and yours had better stay under the blankets for a little while longer.-

-Fiand? Liesel Fiand? - he tries to remember.

-Don't worry about it,- she laughs. He looks upset because he obviously does not remember her. -It was only a short meeting and quite a while ago.-

-I've forgotten so many things,- he murmurs. -Do you know, for a while, I could not even remember my own name, or how I got here, or how old I was? I used to lie here and try to remember things, but the more I tried, the more confused I got. It is a frightening thing.... . I'd try to get up to go to dinner and hope somebody would say something to me, even just greet me maybe, so that I might remember some things. There is a large Italian lady.... . She remembered my name!-

194

As he talks, he becomes more and more excited, and Liesel is afraid that he will wear himself out. -Listen, *Herr* Mann,- she interrupts him. -It is very important that you rest now. I will bring you a drink of juice and, in an hour or so, I'll come back with something light to eat. If you feel up to it then, we'll change your sheets and make you more comfortable, and then we can talk some more. Once you feel a little better, I am sure, you will start remembering.-

She is not at all sure that this is so, but in any event, he must not get too excited. When she returns with his drink a few minutes later, she is glad to see that he is already fast asleep.

Later, Aida and Liesel change his sheets and help him wash, and Doctor Sato stops by during the evening with advice and medication. Despite their every effort, however, it takes several weeks before he is able to get up every day and take part in the regular activities of the house. This gives Liesel time to convince Sister Olga that she is not harboring a traitor, and during the many conversations she has with him while he is convalescing, she becomes more and more certain that he was indeed the innocent victim of a gross injustice.

-Do you know, I have been trying to think what I might have done or said that could have given them the idea I was spying, but I can't for the life of me figure it out,- he says. -I was a resident of the United States at one time before the war, quite a few years ago, though. And then, I was told that they found papers stating that I had money in China. I don't, so why did they say I did? I know that once I made a complaint about the inefficiency of the Tokyo fire department, but surely that does not constitute treason?-

He shakes his head and leans back against the pillows. His white face would completely disappear there, were it not for his flaming beard. He does not want to shave it or even let Aida trim it for him, and Liesel's eyes are invariably drawn to it as she sits there listening to him.

-I know I look like Barbarossa or maybe Rasputin,- he laughs. - But, no matter. I am really more afraid of what I might look like when I shave it off. It's like a mask that I can hide behind.- He closes his eyes and frowns. -Isn't it paradoxical! On the one hand, I want to remember and know all about myself, but on the other hand, I am afraid that maybe I might find out something dreadful.

-There was this one guard in particular; the others were not really so bad. But this fellow was huge and totally bald. He enjoyed kicking us, and he'd cry 'traitor! spy! traitor!' in rhythm with the kicks. It got worse the last few months, just before we were freed. He smoked non stop. Liked to make us stand against the wall, and then he'd stub out his cigarettes on our bare chests. He seemed to have it out for me particularlyy. 'Come tell me, Mann-*san*, what did you tell your American friends about us?' he would jeer. 'It won't help them, no matter what you told them, you traitorous dog! Japan will be victorious! The American cowards are on the run. You will be here a nice long time. Won't you like that? Don't you like our hospitality?'

-In the end, I used to wonder if maybe I had actually turned traitor. He seemed so convinced of it. I thought, maybe I had let something slip inadvertently. But then, I'd wonder what I could have said. I did not know anything!-

196

-Were you surprised when you were finally freed? Or had you suspected that the end was near?- Liesel asks him. He seems to want to talk about it, and she hopes that it will help him come to grips with himself.

-I could not believe it,- he murmurs. -Sometimes I still can't believe that I am actually out of there. I used to dream about it in prison. We slept on the floor in our thin clothes and one blanket each and in winter it was very cold. But when this guy came on duty, he'd make us strip and take away our blankets. And then he'd open the windows. But after being forced to stand at attention most of the day, we were so tired at night that we actually slept. But only an hour at a time usually. He'd come and shine a bright light at us every hour or so, and we'd have to get up and snap to attention again. After the first hour of sleep, we would feel the cold, and often, we wouldn't be able to get back to sleep all night.

-I'd lie there then, in the dark, and dream about being freed. Then, I'd feel like a real traitor, because the only way I could see myself getting out was if the Americans would win the war, and they were supposed to be the enemy. But none of my German or Japanese friends had come forward on my behalf. Help would have to come from the Americans. After a while, I didn't care anymore. I only wanted to get out, no matter how.

-The day before our freedom, I thought this guy would kill us all. I think he tried. If the Americans hadn't come... , I am sure I wouldn't have lasted another day... .-

Liesel sits quietly listening to him talk, but she is afraid that he will go into details about his tortures again. She finds that very hard to listen to, especially since she has seen the wounds on his chest and back. Aida clucked her tongue and swore quietly in Italian when they were helping him get ready for Doctor Sato, but he looked embarrassed by her murmurs of sympathy. He said nothing then, but a few days later he told Liesel about his ordeal. She does not want to hear it again.

Outside, snow is falling. The garden has turned into a winter wonderland, and the children are trying to build a snowman.

-I couldn't believe it when they walked into the cells,- he says. -There was a noise outside the door, and I thought, 'Here he comes again!'. I tried to get up before he opened the door. I wasn't able to get up very quickly anymore by then, and so I used to listen so that I'd have a head start. He'd kick you with his yellow army boots, if you weren't fast enough at standing and saluting. I was facing the door. I had my eyes closed because I was dizzy, but I was standing at attention. And then I heard my name called in a Texas drawl. 'Are you Heinz Mann? Mr. Heinz Mann?' An American officer! He was standing inside the cell. A big guy with a pot belly and a very red face, but at that moment, I swear, I loved every inch of him.

'Yes, I'm Heinz Mann,' I said. He was surprised that I spoke English. 'You're free to go, Mr. Mann,' he said, and when I looked at him, rather stupidly I imagine, he said, 'The war is over, Sir. You're free to go. The charges against you no longer stand. Do you have a place to go?'

-I was so anxious to get out of there, I said that yes, of course, I had a place to go to. And only when I got outside, did I remember that I'd been in there for quite some time, and maybe my place had been bombed and my friends.... Maybe I no longer had any friends.... Kimiko brought me here after a while. She is a good old soul.-

-You have friends now, Heinz Mann,- Liesel tells him. -And that is the most important thing.-

He looks at her and smiles slowly, there are tears in his eyes. -Yes, I have friends now, I know it,- he says.

XVII

I remember his red beard and the blue eyes that twinkled whenever he was planning mischief. He was our Onkel *Heinz, and he read the funnies to us, translating them from English to German. It was more fun than making up our own stories, and we would fight to sit on his lap. I liked to play with his beard, but one day, I asked him if he would shave it off, because* Tante *Aida had said he was a very handsome man, except for that awful red rag. Mama told me to hush, and he laughed. 'What do you think, Liesel?' he asked Mama, 'should I shave it off?' But she only smiled and told him it would have to be his decision, she could not tell him what he should do.*

One day, when Frau *Sacca was late for breakfast, as she almost always was, he suggested that we go up and knock at her door and tell her that breakfast was getting cold and that it was time to get up. It was fun to think about doing that, and we tried hard to convince ourselves that it was indeed a good idea. After all, it was quite late, and she would soon miss lunch as well, if she did not get up now. Maybe she didn't have an alarm clock, and she would be ever so grateful to us for reminding her of the time. We saw ourselves knocking at her door and then making a dash for it to a safe distance. If she opened her door, we would holler, 'It's time to get up now,* Frau *Sacca!' and run for it. It made us feel all queasy inside, just to think about it. But we never did it. Mama told us that* Frau *Sacca was quite capable of looking after herself, and she shook her head at* Onkel *Heinz and told him it was obvious that he was fully recovered. He said that* Frau *Sacca was an 'irresistible temptation to him,' and that he had had a very strict upbringing, and these urges to mischief had never had a proper outlet. And Baerbel and I crept around the house and looked up at* Frau *Sacca's window and wondered what an 'irresistible temptation' was.*

Onkel *Heinz often came after dinner to play* Skat *with* Oma *and Mama, and we would hear them laughing in the big room, while we had to go to sleep. But then one evening I heard him talking to Mama, and* Oma *was not there. And they were not laughing. The next day,* Onkel *Heinz went away to Tokyo, and when he came back a few days later, he said that he had found a job and that he would be away most days. He said that he would not be able to play with us as much as before. And Mama looked sad.*

*****

Heinz Mann is a great favorite with the girls right from the first day they are introduced to him. His beard absolutely fascinates them. Resel, in particular, does not miss a chance to tug at it whenever she is allowed to sit on his lap. When he is stronger, he lets them ride on his back, while he crawls on all fours through the playroom. He tells them adventure stories and listens to their chatter by the hour. He is the first to nickname the twins the 'Katzenjammer Kids' and, in order that they might live up to that name, he dutifully puts them up to many little pranks.

-*Tante* Olga, when are we going to have those delicious oysters that Ryoichi-*san* brought back from his brother's house yesterday?- Baerbel looks at Sister with innocent, questioning eyes.

-What oy... , er, yes, to be sure. Well..., I think we will have them tonight then.- Sister looks puzzled and annoyed and rushes to the kitchen.

-I know we would never have seen them,- Heinz tells Liesel with a grin, when Baerbel innocently reports on her mission. -She would have kept them for herself and sold the rest to the neighbors. Ryoichi told me yesterday that he had brought them as a special treat for the guests here. She is probably wondering now how anyone could possibly have known about those oysters.-

-You are becoming too healthy for your own good,- Liesel tells him. -You need a job to keep you busy and the twins out of trouble.-

He looks at her thoughtfully. -I would not be where I am now if it had not been for you,- he says. -There are hours, even whole days now, when I don't think of prison. I actually think that, in time, I might get over it.- He smiles at her. -I owe you so much... , and the children too. You mean a great deal to me... .-

But that evening, at dinner, he is back to his tricks again. While everyone is enjoying a feast of oysters in the shell, Aida recounts how 'her dear Otto' had once found a pearl in an oyster at a Tokyo restaurant. She is busy recalling his exact expression of surprise and reaction of joy, and no one notices Heinz quietly leaving the table and returning a short while later. Towards the end of the meal, he suddenly lets out a choking sound and jumps up from the table. -It can't be! This is incredible!- he cries, and when he has everyone's attention, he pulls out an entire string of pearls from his mouth, to the great amusement of the entire table.

A few days later, the twins come running into Liesel's room full of excitement. -Mami, come and see *Onkel* Heinz! He looks so different now!- They pull her along the corridor towards the front door. He is there, sitting on the steps, talking to Hannele.   -Look Mami, *Onkel* Heinz has a naked chin now.- Hannele laughs.

He blushes when he sees Liesel's surprise. -It had to go,- he says. -I am sure no one would hire a Rasputin.-

That evening Heinz knocks on Liesel's door while *Oma* is out visiting. He tells her that he thinks he might have a good chance to be hired by the Americans as an interpreter.

-How many languages do you speak, Heinz?- she wants to know.

He shrugs. -Seven, I guess, more or less. Well, then I have a smattering of Chinese as well. So that would make it eight, I suppose.- He is almost apologetic about it. -It isn't so difficult, once you know two or three, and it always helps to live among the people,- he says. -I've been just about everywhere in this part of the world, and when I was a young fellow, I had to travel in Europe for my father's firm. I always had this yearning to see the world, you know. Used to think of myself as a sort of Axel Heyst. Travel about, no lasting involvements, just stand back and observe. That's why I couldn't believe it when they arrested me. I became involved with a vengeance then.- He looks at Liesel with a thoughtful, almost tender smile. - Did you ever read the novel *Victory* by Joseph Conrad?- he asks.

-No, I haven't.- Liesel says. - He is one of Willi's favorite writers though. Why do you ask?-

He doesn't answer right away, but goes to the window and stares out into the night. -The protagonist, Axel Heyst, is a loner, a philosopher really, who doesn't believe in becoming involved in life,- he says finally. -Heyst travels throughout the Orient, never staying in one place very long. And then, he meets a woman and becomes involved. He falls in love with her... .-

He stops and clears his throat, his back to Liesel. -One could say that she brings about his downfall, I suppose... . But I think she is his redemption, really.-

-Why?- Liesel asks quietly. His tone of voice has changed. He stands there, very still, almost as though he were waiting for something.

-Through her, he learns to care about living. To feel. To love,- he says finally.

Liesel does not know what to say. The room is very quiet. She can smell the spring blossoms through the open window. Somewhere a train whistles in the darkness. The clock ticks a toneless rhythm. She looks at Willi's picture on the chest of drawers. -... 'I go back into the past and feel you in my arms again.... Maybe soon now we will be together in the beautiful hills and meadows of home.... Let us direct our thoughts to the future, *mein Herz*, when we will once again be united....' His loving, tender words.....-

Heinz turns and sees her glance. He shakes his head and looks away.

-Heinz.....-

-It's all right, Liesel.- He shakes his head again. -My luck, I guess. Don't feel bad about it. I just wanted you to know.-

-I am so sorry.-

-No need,- he smiles. -We won't talk about it any more. I have no right, I know, and I value your friendship too much. But I feel very strongly about this, and I want to say it. I think you were my redemption, Liesel. You rescued me from the darkness and made me want to live again. I'll always love you for that.- He hugs her to him for a brief moment, and then he leaves the room, very quickly.

Liesel sits for a long time, her face in her hands. Weeping.

***

She does not see him for a few days, and the children want to know where their favorite playmate is. Then, one afternoon, he comes visiting again, grinning from ear to ear. -I start on Monday,- he tells Liesel. -Right at army headquarters. It took a while to find the right person to talk to, but after that, no problem. I'll get most of my meals there as well. It's really quite a nice set up.-

Liesel is painfully surprised that her first reaction is one of loss. He will be busy, meet some interesting people and make new friends, and she will miss him... dreadfully. She may well have been his ticket back to life, but he has been good for her too. He is a kindred spirit, someone with whom she could exchange ideas that were important to her. How long it has been since she has had such a friend! She finds it difficult to hide her initial reaction and is annoyed when she feels herself blush with embarrassment. -Oh..., how very nice for you, Heinz,- she stammers. -I am... ,I'm so glad for you.... We..., er... the children will certainly miss you.-

He smiles at her then. -I'll be here most evenings and weekends, Liesel,- he says. -I hope you don't intend to find another partner for *Skat*.-

The job eventually turns out to have some happy benefits for Liesel as well. The money situation has become very difficult. There simply isn't any. Stamps for food and clothing are provided, but no cash. Everyone has to earn what he or she needs over and above the bare essentials, through whatever means possible, and Liesel has started to sew. Usually that involves remaking remakes, and it doesn't bring in much. Aida is her only good customer. Her husband has left her a small fortune in jewelry and Swiss bank notes, and she is never short of money, and very generous. Liesel also finds that corpulent people seem to require more clothes, and Aida keeps her busy with something or other most of the time.

Not long after he starts working for the Americans, Heinz asks her if she would like to do some sewing for a couple of friends. It seems, whenever the young army men have their shirts or summer jackets laundered, the various military insignia have to be removed, since the method of washing used in their laundry makes the colors run. The men find it a tedious job to sew the insignia on again after each washing.

-They would be very happy if they could find someone to do this for them, and it would pay well,- Heinz tells Liesel.

The next day, he drives up in an army jeep and introduces Liesel to Lieutenants Dick Roberts and Jack McKay. Lieutenant Roberts is from Cleveland, Ohio, and Jack McKay is from Texas. They are tall and very shy, and are obviously relieved when the children run up and they can devote their time to handing out chewing gum and letting Resel and Baerbel ride on their shoulders.

This is the first of many visits. Two or three times a week, they drive up with a box of shirts, their own and those of friends. At the bottom of the box, covered with several layers of shirts to avoid curious stares, Liesel finds several pounds of sugar, chocolates, peanut butter and coffee, in addition to a generous payment in yen.

They soon overcome their shyness with Liesel, and she finds that her English improves rapidly as she listens to their stories from home and other anecdotes. Dick intends to finish his studies in veterinary medicine when he goes back to the States. He also is engaged to be married. Jack is married with two children and will help his father in a grocery business when he goes back home. They are both homesick and feel happy surrounded by children and a homelike environment.

One day, Kaete Zimmermann, back from Hakone, where she had fled during the worst of the bombing, comes by for a visit. Liesel is happy to see her after what seems such a very long time, and she introduces her to her new American friends.

-Do they ever ask you about those awful stories that are coming out of Germany?- Kaete wants to know when the men have left.

-What stories? What is coming out of Germany?- Liesel asks.

-Heavens! I do believe you live like a recluse here in this beehive!- she exclaims. -But then, you don't read the English papers, do you? The stories about the concentration camps at Dachau and Buchenwald and a place called Auschwitz. All those horrible things that are supposed to have happened there. The Jews that were killed.-

-The Jews that were killed? What do you mean? ... Those stories we heard from Bert and Greta Klausner in Surabaya? But they talked about ransacking of stores and beatings in the street, not killing. And Willi did not believe them.- Liesel remembers clearly how uneasy she had felt then.

-From what they say in the papers, Bert's stories were mild in comparison,- Kaete says quietly. -They found mass graves, thousands killed, maybe millions. They don't know how many yet. Not only Jews; the mentally ill, the handicapped, and anyone who opposed the *Reich* in any way. People tortured, burned... .-

Liesel stares at her, speechless. -Oh, my God! How could this happen? In our country? Who did this?- she whispers.

-I don't know. Maybe it isn't true. After-war propaganda, maybe. I keep hoping that it is all a lie. But still... those graves..., those pictures!-

That evening Liesel asks Heinz what he has heard or read. He looks at her, obviously troubled, and shakes his head. -It isn't pretty,- he says. -I didn't want to tell you, because I knew you'd be so upset. I keep hoping that something will come out that will make it less awful.-

-Is it true then? People tortured, mass graves?-

-The American papers are full of it. Pictures, everything. Makes my prison troubles seem like child's play,- he says.

Did the people know? The German people? The everyday people, like you and me? I mean, we here in Japan did not know much about the activities of the Japanese secret police and what they did to people like you in their prisons. Do you suppose this sort of thing went on under cover? Do they say anything about that in the papers? Do they say who did this?- Liesel talks very fast, her voice shaking, distraught. She puts her hand on his arm and shakes it. -Heinz, who is responsible?-

He seems to be in a trance. -Why?- he asks. -What does that matter?- His voice is toneless, and he looks at her with a haunted expression.

-Well, of course it matters!- she cries -If people did not know, how could they be held responsible, and what could they do? I did not know. Willi did not know, and the little we heard seemed so incredible, we could not believe it... .-

-But don't you see?- Heinz interrupts her impatiently. -It seemed incredible, so you and I simply dismissed it as untrue and shut our ears and eyes. Hitler and his ilk had us all screaming for the *Vaterland*. Mass frenzy! That's what it was. I was at the Olympic games in '36. We loved him! ... - He looks at her, his face rigid. -Thousands of boys died screaming '*Heil* Hitler!' But how many do you think it took to guard those camps, round up those victims, fire the gas ovens that killed all those people? How many more who knew or, at least, suspected what their friends, relatives, husbands were doing and kept silent out of fear, a misguided sense of values, God knows why? -

His voice is a mere whisper now. -They died too... , the death of the soul... , the German soul. I tell you, if this is true, and I can't honestly believe that it isn't, then Germany lost far more than lives, homes, industry. This will be a wound that will fester for centuries.-

Liesel stares at him, unable to speak, and he stops abruptly. - I'm sorry. I know you have been away from there for a long time. I should not talk like that. But I was there often during the thirties, when he first came to power. I raised my hand and screamed '*Heil* Hitler!' with the rest of them. Intelligent, educated people. I've thought about it a lot over the last little while, and I believe there is such a thing as blood guilt, even for those who did not lift a finger to aid this slaughter.- He looks at Liesel, but does not see her.

-Sins of omission they call it, don't they?-

That night, Liesel lies awake for a long time, listening to the even breathing of her three little girls in their beds next to hers. -What did Willi write? Those beautiful words. ... 'My belief in the homeland is undaunted.... . Love for the paths of home is the pillar of being.' And it is true. I do believe that. But blind love is no love at all... . Who was it that said, 'There is no light without darkness.'? It's when we try to deny the potential power of evil, no, worse, when we reject even the possibility that it exists; exists in all of us, ...that darkness within, then we are lost. ... 'We must do our part in trying to rebuild our dear homeland.' ...Oh Lord! Will that still be possible now or ever again? -

XVIII

Some years ago, I wrote a poem about death, or rather, the idea of death, which, in mid-life, seems to become an ever increasing presence in one's daily consciousness. I saw it as a shadow, lurking within me, a 'fleeting darkness,' an 'enemy of tranquil thought' which had the power to cast a shadow over my moments of happiness.

Today, I have come to think of the feeling of guilt in a similar manner, or rather, as having a more sinister impact. The thought of death, after all, can have the redeeming factor of making life 'more precious' and 'love more sweet.' But I think that guilt, unlike repentance, can be a useless and even destructive emotion. The dictionary defines it as 'a feeling' of having done wrong. But I see it as a feeling, frequently not justified and not necessarily related to fact. I know it as an insidious thing which creeps into the mind unbidden often without rhyme or reason. I know it, and I know it well, because it is my patrimony and that of all German children of war, the ones who are truly without blame, but who carry within them the blood guilt of a nation. And I cry for innocence, for the love of the hills and the paths of Papa's Heimatland, *which, loving idealist that he was, he held within his heart till the end, but which to me are lost.*

*****

213

Time drags on, and summer is on its way. No preparations appear to be in progress to arrange for the return to Germany of all the women and children still stranded in Japan. Willi writes that the prisoners of war in Dehra Dun are soon to leave for home, and Liesel is becoming increasingly anxious for the future.

Several written appeals by various German groups to the American military government have produced no results, not even the courtesy of a reply. According to Heinz, General MacArthur is supposed to have said: 'They got themselves over here on their own, they can damn well get back by themselves.'

-But how?- she wonders. -If only I could fly!- At night she dreams of flying home, to Willi. And during the day she wonders what home will be like, the old city of Freiburg, surrounded by the beautiful mountains of the Black Forest. Willi's mother has a small place ready for them, which they will share with her and Willi's adopted brother, Johann. Two rooms and a kitchen for seven people.... But they are lucky, many people are living in the cellars of bombed-out houses, happy to have a roof over their heads.

-You will like it there, Liesele,- Willi writes. -*Mutter* is lovable and down to earth, and she is so anxious to make a nice home for us.- He himself has not been home in almost twenty years, and Liesel wonders how he will adjust to the confinement of Germany's rigid bureaucracy. She knows that his soul has always been that of a wanderer, and he told her many years ago, that he had found the attitudes of his hometown too closed and archaic. -His spirit has to soar and fly far.- she thinks. -That is why I love him.-

She keeps busy with her sewing, but the money she makes from that won't buy their passage home. It does, however, keep shoes on little feet, which suddenly seem to grow like weeds.

After her conversation with Heinz about the horrors of the concentration camps, she feels awkward with her American friends, wondering what they might be thinking of her now. She knows that the shame she experiences is unreasonable, since she was far away from Germany at the time, but that does not diminish her feelings of culpability. But Dick and Jack never mention the matter, and after a while, when they continue to be as helpful and friendly as ever, her uneasiness abates somewhat.

It has been several weeks now since she has seen Aida who is frequently out visiting her many Italian friends. Sometimes, Liesel hears her muffled laughter in the hall late at night. She seldom comes to dinner and seems to be avoiding Liesel's rooms. Then, one day, quite unexpectedly, she introduces Liesel to Antonio, and it is evident that she is in love.

He is a small, stocky man with black, curly hair and laughing eyes, and he is very young. His German is limited, but Aida, in her evident desire that Liesel and Antonio become friends, translates his every word, while he nods and smiles his approval.

Liesel's first reaction is one of uneasiness. Aida is a woman in her late-thirties, romantic and rich, while Antonio must have joined the Italian merchant navy when he was barely out of school, for he is certainly not yet twenty-five. He has no trade, and, like many of the German merchant marines, has spent the last years of the war in Japan, helping damsels in distress. Aida spoils him and frets over him, worrying about his every frown. Several times, Liesel is at the point of saying something, but with Aida, that would do no good, and she suspects that he is a very clever young man.

Early one morning, Aida comes to Liesel's room crying. -Antonio says that he won't stay another night. He says that my Otto gives him the shudders,- she sobs, forgetting completely about the impropriety of Antonio's having stayed the night with her in a family boarding house.

-Does he know how strongly attached you are to your er... , well, to your, your Otto?- Liesel asks gently.

-That's just it!- she cries. -He tells me that I cannot love two men. It is either Otto or Antonio. And if it is Antonio, then Otto has to go, or else he will never come back, never!- She is close to hysteria.

-Where is Antonio now, Aida?-

-He left just now. Stormed right out of the room and slammed the door! Did you not hear it?-

Liesel makes her a cup of coffee, and the two women sit quietly for a few minutes while Aida's tears flow freely.

216

-Aida, you must decide whether you truly love Antonio... -

-Love? Love? I adore him, Lisa! I adore this man! I cannot keep my hands.... . I, oh, I have never felt like this , never!-

-And he probably knows it,- Liesel thinks and just barely stops herself from saying it out loud. It would do no good to turn Aida against her, if she wants to help her in any way. But that looks like a formidable task indeed.

-Aida, that sort of feeling does not always last. He is asking you to choose. Has he made any promises that entitle him to demand this of you?- she asks as kindly as possible.

-He loves me,- Aida answers between sobs. -He says he adores me, and he wants to marry me.-

-And do you want to marry him?-

She stares ahead, not saying anything for a minute. -I need a man, Lisa. I did not know how much. I do not want to be a widow all my life. And I do not want to go home to Italy alone. I am not so young now, anymore... .-

-But Aida, you have still so much of your life ahead of you! You are an attractive woman! There will be plenty of opportunities to get married in Italy. Take your time! Look around! Don't let yourself be pushed into this.... .- Liesel stops abruptly. That was the wrong thing to say. Aida is frowning.

-I love Antonio,- she says with determination. -I am not being pushed, as you say.- Her chin juts out stubbornly, and Liesel knows she has lost. Maybe she is judging Antonio prematurely. After all, what does she know of him, really? It's just a hunch, that's all, and that's not fair to him, is it?

-I should not have bothered you,- Aida says and gets up.

Liesel puts a hand on her friend's arm . -You did not bother me, Aida,- she says quietly. -You were unhappy, and I don't like to see you that way.-

Tears start flowing again, and Aida buries her face in her hands. -What will I do about Otto?- she sobs.

-Let's ask Father Joseph at the Jesuit mission.- Liesel suggests. -He will know what to do.-

A few days later, Liesel and Aida attend a private interment service at the Jesuit chapel. Aida now has a tiny urn, which she keeps under lock and key. Only she and Liesel know about it. The rest of her beloved Otto is placed in hallowed ground in the Jesuit cemetery. The wedding is scheduled to take place within days.

The evening before the ceremony, Aida comes to Liesel's room looking worried and begins to cry again when Liesel asks her why she is so obviously upset.

-Lisa, I have been thinking,- she stammers. -It is silly, maybe, I suppose, but you know about Otto.... When we are called to heaven, in the end, you know, the big day of the judgment, what will happen with Otto, if he is here, and a little part of him is in Italy?-

-Poor soul! She is still worried about her Otto,- Liesel thinks. -I certainly hope that Antonio will be worthy of her!- She smiles at Aida. -I think that the dear Lord will have no problem putting things together in the end,- she says. -Place and time won't matter then, Aida, only love. And you have a heart full of it. That's all that ever counts with God.-

The wedding celebration is a boisterous affair. Heinz and Liesel are invited, of course. He speaks Italian fluently and gets along famously, but Liesel feels quite lost. Her heart aches for Aida with a dull premonition.

-You are not enjoying yourself,- Heinz says. It is a statement, not a question. Liesel looks at him and then over at Aida. -Yes, I see,- he mutters. -I did not want to say anything, but I see we agree anyway. For her sake, I hope we are both wrong.- He follows Liesel's eyes to the smiling couple who are being toasted for the twentieth time.

When Aida and Antonio come back from their honeymoon, she moves away from Olga House, and Liesel rarely sees her. A short time later, the Italian marines suddenly have a chance to leave Japan, but because of her former marriage, Aida's papers cannot be put in order in time. Liesel hears that Antonio is leaving with the others 'to prepare a home in Italy.' But not before Aida has changed her Swiss bank accounts to his name.

***

Tokyo in summer is an experience! For three weeks in early July, the temperatures hover around 36C, and there is no change in sight. Even nighttime brings no relief. The children are pale and sickly. Liesel suspects that the starvation diet in Takedao has lowered their resistance. Resel and Baerbel suffer frequent black-outs from the heat, and by the end of July, Liesel is at her wit's end.

When *Oma* receives an unexpected letter from Wilma urging her to come to Hakone for a visit, she offers to take the twins with her for a holiday in the mountains. -And when you finish your sewing, Liesel, you can come up yourself and fetch them back,- she suggests.

It seems like a god-sent solution, but Liesel is not so sure that she wants to send the twins to stay with Wilma. *Oma,* however, is convinced that she will be able to take care of things and eventually persuades Liesel not to worry. - It is only for a few weeks, and it will give you a reason to visit Hakone.- she says. -You might like it yourself and decide to stay on.-

Liesel has a feeling that *Oma* is a little afraid herself of suddenly being alone with a daughter she has not seen for years and who has always been unpredictable. However, while Hannele does not seem to mind the heat, the twins definitely need to get away to a cooler climate. So for the moment, she really does not have a choice but to accept *Oma's* offer.

The twins are excited about their trip, but when the time comes to say good-bye, they are not so anxious to go, and Liesel sees their little white handkerchiefs waving out of the train window long after she is sure they can no longer see her waving back. As she leaves the station, her uneasiness returns. -Maybe it would not be such a bad idea to move up there,- she wonders. She knows that Hakone has an ever-increasing German population. -It might just be the place to live until a passage home can be arranged.-

Kaete Zimmermann has her own opinion about Hakone. She had preferred to return to Tokyo as soon as she could after the war. -There is no doubt that it is probably one of the most beautiful spots in all of Japan. The mountains, the crystal clear lake and the Fuji overlooking all.- she says. -You simply can't believe it is real when you see it…. But I just didn't like the atmosphere.

-Does *Oma* know that Wilma is having an affair with this Teddy What's-His- Name?- She pulls a face and laughs. -You know, I simply can't remember that man's last name. Everybody always calls him Teddy. I've yet to figure out if that's because he is so short and clumsy, like a real teddy bear, or because of all that hair.-

-Hair?- Liesel asks.

-Yes, I never saw a man with so much body hair! Right up his neck and down to his finger tips. And his arms are longer than any other part of him. When you see him, you can have no doubts about the theory of evolution.- She stops and grins mischievously at Liesel. -Oh, I know you hate it when I talk about people that way, but it is therapeutic, you know. You ought to try it sometime. I really can't imagine what she sees in him though. When I think of Hans, it makes me so angry!-

-Hans is dead.- Liesel reminds her. -Wilma is a widow now.-

-Yes, I know.- Kaete sighs. -And so am I. But I still can't see it. Oh, I know it's none of my business. Anyway, Hans or no Hans, that never made the slightest difference to Wilma, and you know it. Besides, that Teddy has a wife and two children in Bremerhafen.-

-What worries me is her sudden change of attitude towards her mother,- Liesel murmurs thoughtfully. -There is something strange here. I know Wilma…. Well, let's hope I'm wrong. We'll see when I go to get the twins next week.-

-I thought you said that you might stay there,- Kaete says. y-As I said, it's an absolutely gorgeous place, and maybe you won't mind the people so much.- She shrugs, -If you were there, it might be bearable. I could probably stand it myself then. Anyway, I'd be tempted to try. But one odd ball against the crowd is a bit much.-

-You mean, with me there, that would make it two odd balls, is that it? You and I? Thanks a lot.- Liesel laughs.

-They call it sin-city, you know.- Kaete's eyes gleam with laughter. -Really, they do! Irma Kaufman is up there too. You remember her from Sarangan? She lives with the local doctor now. A blond, Nordic type. I forget his name. He is certainly nicer than her Fritz ever was, and he is good to Annegrete. Everyone has someone up there. Christa Braun lives with a resident German, a geologist, Doctor Feld, I believe. He has been in Japan for many years and lives and acts like a Japanese. They think that if you have come through the war without an affair, there must be something wrong with you, and they don't hesitate to tell you so.-

Kaete shakes her head. -I remember when I was there, I had trouble once with a leaking faucet in the bathroom. I tried to fix it myself. Getting a plumber was next to impossible then. But after I had gotten drenched a couple of times, I asked one of the men to help me. Later, his girlfriend told me that if I needed help, I should get my own man. She was not prepared to share.-

-Sounds like a fun place, - Liesel groans.

-In every sense of the word!- Kaete chuckles, and then, suddenly, in one of her quick mood changes, she murmurs quietly, -Oh Liesel, I know it's true. Life is easier with a man around. And loneliness is so darn hard to bear! Lord, when I think of the past five years! If Bernt had been here, nothing would have mattered, it seems to me. We could have faced it together. But I don't think there will ever be a Bernt again. Not for me anyway. It took me almost thirty years to find him. What chance do I have to find another one like him?- Her lips tremble, and she stops talking.

-You are still young, Kaete,- Liesel tries to console her. -I had it happen to me once, you know. Someone I loved dearly died, and I thought that was the end for me. But I found Willi after that. Many years later, to be sure, but it was even more wonderful then.-

-Well, maybe… .- Kaete says doubtfully. - But you're a lot prettier than I am. At any rate, I'm not counting on anything.-

Oma's letters are very enthusiastic. The place reminds her of Sarangan, she writes. What a spot for a good hotel! There are plenty of places for rent, and Liesel should seriously consider moving up there. She says that Hakone had been picked as the site for the Olympic games that were to have been held in Japan but were cancelled because of the war. There are several houses in the mountains, serviced by a good, paved road. They had been intended to house the athletes but have never been used, and the present owners are anxious to rent them for practically nothing, before they fall into complete disrepair. Wilma wants to move from her present place to something more private and would like it if her mother and Liesel would share one of these houses with her.

Liesel decides to go and have a look. When she tells Heinz about her plan, he arranges with Jack McKay to have them driven up to Hakone by jeep. The place is very popular with the Americans. Fishing is good in Lake Hakone, and almost every weekend, there is an influx of military men who rent the local sailing boats, row boats, or anything else that floats. They frequent the few poorly serviced restaurants and are generally out to have a good time. Heinz has often been there lately and confirms Kaete's claim about the climate and the scenery.

-That place is a gold mine for anyone with a bit of money to start a good hotel or even a half decent restaurant,- he says, and Liesel tells him laughingly that she can see dollar signs in his eyes.

-No, not for me!- he answers, and then, looking at her with that strange, searching look of his, he adds, -I won't be here much longer, Liesel. They are trying to get me a visa for the States. Dick Roberts has influential friends in Washington, it seems. If it comes through, I'm on my way.-

Liesel feels her heart drop at the thought of losing him. Kaete is right, life is so much easier when you are not all alone, and Heinz has been such a good friend. But she had not been able to give him any more than friendship, and he had never demanded more, though she knows that it had not been easy for him.

-Heinz, I am glad for you, but I shall miss you,- she tells him quietly.

He reaches out his hand and touches her cheek. -If you asked me, I would stay,- she reads in his eyes.

-I shall surely miss you,- she says again, and her heart breaks because she is causing him pain. She quickly turns her face away, so that he won't see the look in her eyes and misinterpret it.

-Thank you for that much, Liesel,- he says, and squeezes her hand until it hurts.

He has to work the weekend Liesel and Hannele plan to drive to Hakone, and so Jack McKay and a young officer they do not know are their chauffeurs for the day. But Heinz promises that if she decides to move, he will help her with the trunks the following week. -It will be your last move in Japan,- he smiles. - I think things are finally beginning to look up. You and your Willi will be together before long.-

XIX

The Fujiyama watches over Hakone, and there is no sentinel more magnificent. From dark green foothills rises this hazy, purplish-blue giant, gradually turning to snowy white, perpetual snow its eternal crown. In the evening a pink cluster of clouds adorns the crest of the mountain like a wreath of cherry blossoms. Captured on canvas, no one would believe such beauty possible, but once you have seen it, you will never forget it!

Hakone is surrounded by mountains, and the lake is a glassy jewel in the midst of all this greenery. The little house we were sharing with Oma, Tante *Wilma and her friend lay snugly cradled in a small hollow about half way up one of these mountains. 'Baldy' is what we called our mountain, because it seemed to be the barest of all the peaks around us, though there was plenty of foliage around our house, and the little private path that provided a shortcut to Hakone-Machi was half overgrown with bushes. But behind us, the top of the mountain was bare and windswept, a bleak greenish-yellow semicircle, that always looked lonely.*

We were told that the mountains surrounding the lake had once been the sites of numerous castles, the strongholds of long-ago warlords, and we children, roaming the woods around our house, came across meadows of lilies of the valley,

227

bordered by magnificent bushes of pink and purple azaleas. Mama said they were surely the remains of the parks that once had surrounded ancient castles. And indeed, an old wooden marker in the middle of the forest, bearing Japanese script, was said to be the last remnant of a once magnificent fortress.

The more Japanese section of Hakone, known as Hakone-Machi, situated at the foot of our mountain, was separated by a green belt from its more modern sister town, Moto-Hakone, which housed most of the European population. The two were connected by a long allée *running along the lake and lined with ancient trees, some of which were believed to be a thousand years old. The entrances to both Hakone-Machi and Moto-Hakone were each marked by a large red* torii, *a rather ornate Japanese archway.*

Near our house were several empty houses, most of them partially destroyed by wind and rain, and my fondest memories of our stay in Hakone are related to our childhood adventures exploring these abandoned sites and the woods beyond, inventing stories of samurai *that roamed the meadows and forests long ago.*

Baerbel and I walked to Moto-Hakone three times a week, down the steep little mountain path from our house and along the tree-lined avenue by the lake, to a private school held in the living-room of a not so efficient German lady who had lots to say but little patience. Mama wanted us to be able to read when we arrived in Germany, but unlike Hannele, who had learned to read by herself by the time she was four, Baerbel and I had no interest in books or learning and much rather climbed trees and played wild games in the woods. It was a painful experience, this, our first encounter with formal education, and after a while and many tears, Mama finally gave in and let us enjoy a last year of freedom, before the blackboards and the strap in the crowded classrooms of post-war Germany.

*****

As promised, Heinz helps move Liesel's belongings from Saginomia to Hakone during the third week of August. Sister Olga is not happy about the move, but she knows that Liesel and the children will soon be leaving Japan and that a parting is inevitable. Liesel promises to write and to visit when she can.

Wilma and *Oma* have already moved their belongings into the little Olympic athletes' house, situated half-way up the winding road from Hakone-Machi, when the large jeep, filled to capacity with trunks and suitcases, rolls into the yard. They had agreed to take the smaller, six-*tatami* bedroom near the kitchen, which is separated from the children's and Liesel's larger, eight-*tatami* room by a long, airy living room with an attached sunporch. However, when she moves her belongings into the house, Liesel finds that Teddy has also made the move and that *Oma,* now relegated to the living room, is clearly not happy about this arrangement. Liesel is sure that she has been hoping Wilma would leave her *paramour* behind when she moved. She suspects that this was one of the reasons *Oma* insisted that she come and live with them.

-Teddy was unable to keep his room in Moto-Hakone,- Wilma says when she sees Liesel's questioning look. -And so, I told him that I was sure you would not object if he stayed with us for a while. Mother says that she does not mind sleeping in the living room. She's used to it anyway, isn't she?- The look she gives Liesel dares her to find fault.

-We only had two rooms in Saginomia,- Liesel says quietly.

-Well, this is ever so much roomier then, isn't it? So you can't possibly mind Teddy. Anyway, you know how I hate to sleep alone,- she laughs. -Teddy keeps me warm.- She does not bother to lower her voice when she says this, and later, Liesel overhears the girls discussing the situation as they watch Teddy and Heinz bring in suitcases from the jeep.

Hannele, who does not know Teddy, is obviously puzzled by his presence. -Why is he here?- she asks the twins, frowning.

-Oh, he belongs to *Tante* Wilma,- Resel tells her, feeling important. -She says that she always has cold feet at night, and so she has him sleep with her to keep her warm, kind of like a hot-water bottle.-

Hannele scowls and turns away. -I don't like him,- she says.

-Oh, but he is ever so much nicer than *Tante* Wilma,- Baerbel explains. -Resel and I hated it up here without you and Mami, and *Tante* Wilma was always putting us to bed before it was even dark. But Teddy was nice. He used to sneak us some candy when we were in bed and he knew we were crying.-

-Oh, dear! Why did I send them up here alone?- Liesel mutters to herself. -I should have known they would not be happy. God knows what they have seen or heard!- She feels like turning around and driving back to Saginomia. -What did I let myself in for up here?-

-Don't worry, Liesel.- Heinz tells her, when he sees her unhappy expression. -Give it a try, and if it doesn't work out, Tokyo is only a few hours drive from here. We can always think of something.-

-But you are going away soon to America !- Liesel thinks. -And who will I turn to then?-

He promises to come up soon for a visit. -You might find the food situation a bit more difficult here,- he says. -Some of the merchants are rather fed up with the European take-over of Hakone, and they won't honour the food stamps anymore. Just remember always to take the girls along. They won't turn you down then.- His eyes smile at her. -Dick and I will be up with a few goodies as soon as possible.-

After Heinz leaves, Liesel remembers what Kaete had said. 'Two oddballs in a crowd are better than one.' She decides then and there to look for a place with Kaete as soon as possible.

***

Autumn is on its way, and the hills and mountains around the lake are a multitude of colours. Dick says that the only other places he has seen so beautiful in autumn are the New England States and

Canada. -They have a lot of maple trees there too and fall is something to see. My mother comes from Canada, and we used to visit her folks during Indian summer.- He laughs, when Liesel looks puzzled. -That's what they call the last spell of nice, warm weather up there, just before the snow starts.-

Heinz and Dick take the children sailing during the afternoon, and for supper that evening, they have brought steaks to fry outside. - There is talk that at least one ship of Germans will be leaving shortly,- Heinz tells Liesel. -They haven't decided who will go first, but they are making out the lists now.-

Liesel's heart pounds, and she turns pale. -Can it be true, really true? Maybe we'll be home for Christmas!- In his last letter, Willi wrote that he hoped to be home in early spring. -Maybe, we'll be there to greet him!- she thinks.

-Don't get your hopes up too much,- Heinz cautions, as he is leaving. -Maybe I should not have mentioned it.- He has seen her reaction to his news and worries that she might be disappointed. -I have an inkling that this first ship will probably take mainly resident Germans. They were here long before the war and have been putting pressure on at headquarters. That's what's needed to get action, and they know it. I think it will be the residents and probably the marines, but I wanted you to be ready just in case. They won't allow any valuables, jewelry and that sort of thing, on board. God knows why.- His blue eyes twinkle. -I thought I'd mention it. I know you have experience in situations such as that.-

Well, I haven't much left,- Liesel laughs. -My ring, by some miracle, and a few odds and ends.-

***

Rumors begin to spread in Moto-Hakone, as the news of a possible departure becomes known. It is purely a guessing game, but everyone pretends to know more than anyone else. Wilma has been in a dreadful mood ever since Heinz mentioned the possibility of transportation home. She stays in bed until noon most days, and Liesel frequently hears muffled arguments with Teddy through the thin, parchment-paper walls. He is nervous and grumpy himself most of the time now, and the atmosphere in the house is far from pleasant.

One morning, after a lot of noise and a stormy departure by Teddy, the children are outside playing, and *Oma* decides to visit acquaintances living about half a mile away. The house is empty. Only Wilma is still in bed as usual. Liesel decides that this is as good a time as any to properly hide her few remaining valuables. -The fewer people that know about it, the better,- she thinks. -Then only I can be held responsible, and what the children don't know, they won't talk about.-

She has a large cloth bag with wooden handles, which she uses as a handbag. After some consideration, she makes up her mind to hide her ring and a few small pieces of jewelry in the cloth part of the handbag that fastens onto the wooden handles. She carefully opens both sides of the bag at the inside of the handles and lines the opening with a thin layer of cotton wadding. In this soft protection, between the cloth and the wooden handle, she hides her jewelry.

She is in the process of resewing her handbag, when she hears a sudden gulping noise, and Wilma stumbles out of her room and makes a dash for the washroom. She looks deathly ill, and Liesel rushes after her to see what could be the matter. When she catches up with her, Wilma is leaning her forehead against the cool wall by the sink, groaning.

-God, I hate this mess! What a damn, stupid mess to be in!- she mutters furiously.

-What is the matter? Can I do anything, Wilma? Let me help you back to bed.-

-What earthly good would that do?- she snaps. -You want to do something? Help me get rid of this thing! Lord Almighty! All these years, nothing, and now all of a sudden!- She sees Liesel staring at her. -I'm pregnant! Don't tell me you didn't expect it! Everyone else did, I'm sure!-

-Pregnant?-

-Yes, pregnant! Can't you hear Hans laughing up there? Pregnant! Me, who never wanted his child! And that son of a bitch, Teddy, is leaving me! Taking the first boat home to Germany to his dear little Annemarie and their kiddies.-

-How do you know that? How do you know Teddy is among the ones going?-

-All the marines are going. They heard last night. Oh, how he used to promise he'd divorce her and marry me. That was months ago, after we heard that Hans had died, and he wanted so desperately to hop into the sheets with me. But now it's a different story! He lands me with a kid and then takes off!-

They are in the kitchen now, and Wilma is smashing around the only coffee pot and a precious cup from a set of four cheap china ones that Liesel was able to wrangle from a shopkeeper for a fortune.

-That damn hypocrite! Why do you suppose I'd leave Moto-Hakone to move to this god forsaken spot? Can't you see them smirking down there?- She leads the way to the living room.

- So that was it! She wanted her mother back to be nursemaid, and me, if need be, to do the work around the place. We are not in Surabaya now, and there aren't any *babus* to be had at the drop of a hat... .- It all falls into place now, and Liesel can only blame herself for her own stupidity. Too late she remembers her crafty little handiwork, left unattended in the living room.

-What's this?- Wilma asks and picks up the cloth bag. She gives Liesel a curious stare and flops down on a chair. -I didn't notice that it needed fixing,- she says. But her attention is soon back to her own troubles.

-Mother doesn't know yet, I don't imagine?-

-How could she, unless you told her?- Liesel asks. -You don't show yet. How far along are you?-

-My fifth month,- she groans. -That horse doctor down in Moto-Hakone wouldn't do anything about it by the time I had the nerve to tell anyone.-

Liesel tries her best to cheer her, but there is little she can say. She thinks of Hans and how much he had wanted a child. And now Wilma will have a little one that no one really wants. But nature works in strange ways, and maybe, once she sees it, she will love it. One can only hope.

That evening, one of Teddy's friends comes up to fetch his trunk. It seems that Teddy is not prepared for another confrontation with Wilma, and the ship is leaving in less than two weeks.

-Teddy wants you to have the pearl necklace he bought and that silver brooch,- the fellow tells Wilma, and when she questions him further, he admits that no one is allowed to take valuables on board.

-Isn't he generous now!- she laughs bitterly. -I suppose he hasn't the nerve to try to hide the stuff and take it anyway. No, he wouldn't do that, he'd shake all over! Poor Teddy!-

***

All the resident Germans are leaving, and Moto-Hakone will be a quiet place after their departure. Crista Braun is losing her geologist. Of all the German men, only the doctor is remaining.

-There won't be another ship for several months. Maybe not till next summer now,- Kaete tells Liesel, when she is up to have a look at the little house Liesel has picked out for them. -I'll move up in early spring,- she says. -Wilma will have had her baby by then, and you won't have to feel bad about leaving them.- She looks in the direction of Wilma's room. -Who knows, this might just make a human being out of her, but I doubt it.-

Just before the departure of the *General Black* with its first instalment of Germans, Liesel has a pleasant surprise when Baerbel comes running into the house full of excitement. -Mr. Hendrickson is here, Mami! And Frau Tonne, with a big boy. They are coming up the path!- She is always the first to spot visitors, because her favorite place is half-way up the large maple that grows in the front yard.

-I see you have your own lookout tower, fully staffed,- Sven laughs as he comes in. –We wanted to surprise you.-

Else hugs Liesel, and then, holding out her hand, she says a little shyly, -You remember Karl?- He has grown so tall that Liesel would not have recognized him. Gone is the angry, stubborn look in his eyes, and he is actually embarrassed as he shakes hands.

-*Guten Tag, Frau* Fiand,- he says, blushing.

Liesel makes tea, and they sit on the front porch for a long chat. It is hard to believe that a year has pased since they said goodbye at Takaratzka. Sven, Else and Karl are preparing to leave with the resident Germans on the *General Black*. Sven, who has been working most of the past year with the American military, was able to pull some strings and get passage for Else and Karl as well as for himself.

-It won't be long now for you either,- Else says. She knows how much Liesel wants to leave. –Sven says that, since they have provided a ship for one group, they'll have to do the same for the others sooner or later. It's just a matter of time.-

-It wouldn't hurt to keep writing and maybe to send a delegation to MacArthur,- Sven advises. –It's harder to say 'no' to a person than to a letter. From what I hear, he's not all that bad a fellow and could be persuaded to play the 'knight in shining armour' for a few hundred women and children in distress.-

They are planning to stay with Else's parents and then to leave for Norway as soon as Else can obtain the necessary papers.

-Juergen wrote to say he is going back to Borneo if he can. But I haven't heard from him in almost a year now,- Else tells Liesel, when Sven and Karl have gone out for a moment to admire Baerbel's tree house. –I never wrote him about a divorce, you know. Somehow I didn't feel it was the right thing to do while he was still in detention and all that. But evidently he can't care less even about Karl, since he is determined to go back to Borneo and must know that we can't possibly join him there now. I am going to start divorce proceedings as soon as I get to my parents' place in Hanover.-

-How does Karl feel about it?- Liesel asks. —He and Sven seem to get along fine.-

-Oh, Liesel! He is a changed boy! I don't know how it happened, or why, but he actually seemed glad to see me again. I couldn't believe it! And he likes Sven! I am so happy, Liesel. I only hope it lasts. I can't help thinking that something will surely happen to make things go wrong again.-

Liesel takes her hand. —No, Else, it will be all right from now on. You must have a little faith. Surely you have had your share of suffering. I predict a golden future.- She smiles at Else, and with all her heart, she wishes her only happiness.

-Well, think of me sometimes, Liesel,- she says, when they are leaving. —And pray for me, as I will for you.-

***

At the beginning of December, Heinz Mann suggests a Saint Nicholas visit to Saginomia. During the war, one of the Jesuit fathers always dressed up as Saint Nicholas, the holy bishop who comes to the houses on December 6th to bring apples and nuts to all good children. He is usually supposed to bring his helper, Ruprecht, along, a dark, ominous fellow with a big sack into which he stuffs any child that has been especially bad all year and carries him or her away to an awful place which is never fully defined. But Liesel has never quite approved of Ruprecht ever since the Christmas when he carried away her favorite brother, Jochen, and she cried all during the evening's festivities only to find Jochen sound asleep in his bed when she went up to her room that night. And so the Jesuit fathers omit Ruprecht when they come to Saginomia and stress the happy nature of Saint Nicholas rather than the frightening one.

Sister Olga is happy to see Liesel and the girls again, and the evening is a huge success. Father Joseph from the mission is Saint Nicholas, and when he walks in, in full bishop's regalia, Dick Roberts and Jack McKay almost drop the glasses of punch they are holding. They had expected an American Santa and didn't quite know what to do with a bishop. Heinz, who had forgotten the American custom, quickly whispers an explanation, whereupon both officers relax and, when questioned whether they have been good boys, gravely answer, 'Yes, holy man.'

On Christmas Eve, Liesel and the girls go to an evening service in Hakone-Machi and walk home the long way through the beautiful mountain scenery, amid softly falling snow.

-Next year, we will be with Papa,- Hannele says, tightly holding Liesel's hand.

-Yes, next year, we will be with Papa,- the twins echo, followed by the inevitable demand, -Tell us about Papa, Mami.-

So she tries to tell them about the man she loves, the man who is their father, but whom they do not know. About his smile, and the way he likes to sing. How he knows more than a hundred German folk-songs, many of which he learned while sitting around campfires on hiking trips through the mountains of his beloved Black Forest. How he likes to play the accordion, and how he could dance and tell stories. She tells them, for at least the twentieth time, about the night they met at a concert in Surabaya, a charity affair, and how he had sat in the front row and never taken his eyes off her and, after the performance, had asked her to dinner.

They have heard all this so many times, but they never seem to grow tired of hearing it again. The colour of his eyes; how tall he is; whether he can build playhouses; whether he knows how to drive a jeep.

'Tell them about me, Liesele,' he had asked in his letters. 'And tell them that I love them.' He has missed so much already.... Hannele will be nine in the spring, and Baerbel and Resel will be seven. The twins were six weeks old when he was taken from them.

***

Wilma's time is very close at hand now. She is quieter now that Teddy is gone, and she spends much of her time knitting for the baby. But the children seem to bother her more and more, and she scolds them for the slightest thing. They are not happy in this atmosphere, and Liesel decides that she will move as soon as the baby is born.

One windy February day, Heinz drives up with Dick Roberts. - We have come to say good-bye, *Frau* Fiand!- Dick cries cheerfully as he enters the house. Liesel looks at Heinz, and her heart aches when their eyes meet.

-My visa has come through,- he says. His voice sounds husky. - We are flying to New York the day after tomorrow.- He clears his throat. Liesel finds it hard not to burst into tears.

-Oh, Heinz, that is so very nice for you,- she says. Her voice too sounds funny – the same husky quality.

They have brought some steaks and a bottle of wine for a farewell dinner, but Liesel cannot swallow a bite, and the wine tastes sour. When they are leaving, she runs to the kitchen for a glass of water. Everyone is out by the jeep where Dick is rummaging around for some forgotten chocolate bars.

Then, suddenly, Heinz is there beside her. -Liesel,- he says, -I cannot leave like this.-

She looks at him, and there are tears in her eyes. He stretches out his hands to her. -Let me hold you,- he says. -Just for a moment, let me hold you.- She puts her arms around him then and leans her head against his chest. … He is so tall! …

-I love you,- he says. -You know that I love you!-

She nods. -I know, Heinz, I know… , and… I want to thank you for… for being such a friend to me, when I could not be more to you.- She looks up and smiles through her tears. -When

242

things are better, you will have to come to Germany, to Freiburg, to visit us.-

He bends down and kisses her on the lips, very tenderly, and then he pulls her close and holds her so tightly that she can hardly breathe. -I'll do that, Liesel. You can count on me. I want to meet that Willi of yours, and I want to tell him what a lucky fellow he is.-

XX

Kaete has moved into her little house, and we plan to join her in a few weeks. Wilma had a boy the end of February. She named him Hans. For the christening she invited most of Moto-Hakone. Her bad temper has evaporated and she is everybody's friend now. I don't know where she was able to obtain the provisions for her big party, or how she paid for them, but she told me that money was no problem, since she had sold the jewelry Teddy had left her. An American had wanted something to take home to his wife, she said, and had paid good money for it.

I decided today that I might as well start wearing Willi's ring again, since we could easily be here for several more months. But the ring is gone. The little hollow it had made in the cotton wadding was still there, and so were the few other pieces of jewelry. But the ring is gone. Whoever took it, had not even bothered to resew the opening with the same color of thread. I am surprised that I did not notice it before. I feel sick to my stomach. Only one person could have guessed my hiding place. That person also knows how much that ring meant to me.

This evening I will tell Oma that I have decided to move out right away. Her place is with Wilma now, and I am sorry for her, but I will no longer stay here. There is a limit to everything.

April 1947, Hakone

Spring in Hakone is beyond belief. The cherry blossoms are in bloom and lilies of the valley bloom all around us. The girls roam the meadows and woods and come home, their arms laden with flowers.

Hannele has found a quiet little spot in the woods nearby and spends her time reading everything she can find, but Baerbel and Resel prefer to climb trees. I have decided to let them enjoy these last few months in Japan and will worry about their schooling when we are home in Germany. In any event, Frau Zingraf has thrown in the towel and declared her school experiment a failure. The twins are ecstatic.

May 1947, Hakone

Willi is home in Freiburg. They held him in some sort of British detention center near Hamburg for a while, but now he is home, safe, in Freiburg, and he is working for the French occupation forces. Our home and our love is waiting for us! When, oh when, can we finally go home?

Kaete is one of the committee who has an appointment with General MacArthur, the middle of June. It has taken this

*long just to get an interview with him, and we are told that
we are indeed lucky that he has even agreed to see us. He
seems determined to forget that we exist! I feel so completely
frustrated with no papers, no money, and no means of getting
any, simply at the mercy of someone else's whim. Oh, God!
Please make him see that we surely must get home!*

――――――――――――――

We heard that The General Black *is back in port at Yokohama.
Could it not make a second trip to Germany, this time with
us on board?*

――――――――――――――

*Kaete is back from her interview with MacArthur. She has
no definite news. Just shrugged her shoulders and said that
they will let us know in due course. They were given the
run-around, she said. Lots of talk and lots of red tape.*

*So we continue to wait and pray. Time drags on and on and
on.... Dear Lord, help me to be patient!*

<u>*August 1947, Hakone*</u>

We are leaving Japan! We are going home!

The General Black *will take us at the end of this month! We
are going home to Germany at last!*

Maybe in future years I will look back and remember and maybe even wish to see all this again under different circumstances and not alone. But right now, I cannot envisage that. In August, the month of my birth and yours, mein Herz, *I am coming home at last. I am coming home to you!*

******

The General Black, a gray monster, with hundreds of portholes staring down at the arriving crowd of passengers, looms up into the dark August night. The arrival of the Hakone contingent of women and children has been delayed by the late departure of the trucks and buses, as well as by a thousand-and-one stops along the way for just as many reasons. It is close to midnight now, and the children are barely able to stand on their feet.

-Where is the ship, Mami?- Baerbel wants to know, yawning hugely.

-It's right in front of you, *Schatzi.* Look up there, way up high. Do you see the American soldier up there?-

-That's a ship? Looks more like a big gray wall with holes in it. And he is a toy soldier. How do we get into the ship, Mami?-

-Right over here, ladies! Come this way, please.- A cheerful-looking marine leads the way up the gang-plank. -You are one of the last groups to arrive.-

-Look, Mami! Four beds, right on top of each other! I am sleeping on the very highest one!- Baerbel, followed closely by Resel, makes a dash for the top of the four-layer bunk bed. *The General Black* is a troop-transport. There are only a few private cabins for high-ranking officers. Everyone else has to sleep in huge dormitories with twenty-five beds each. Twenty-five four-layer bunk beds that is, with no guardrails, and the top bunk, right under the ceiling lights, which are only dimmed at night but never fully turned off.

The temperature in Yokohama Harbor is close to 30C even this late at night, but in the dormitory, it is closer to 38C. Rather than argue with the girls, Liesel lets them investigate their chosen sleeping quarters, and it doesn't take long before first Resel and then Baerbel decides that maybe the third layer would be more comfortable and then the second. By the time they are finally asleep, they are in the bottom bunks, Hannele and Liesel in the beds above them and the suitcases on the third layer, which had been Liesel's plan all along.

Though the upper bunks are almost all empty, the dormitory seems over-crowded and noisy. Several fans are going at top speed, but they do not seem to cool the air. People are shifting restlessly. Someone is snoring, and a little child, obviously frightened by that sound, is whimpering for its mother.

-Well, I've traveled better,- Liesel thinks. -But then, who cares. We are going home!-

All the next morning, huge cranes lift luggage into the belly of the ship. Liesel and the girls spend the day investigating the living quarters which will be their home for at least a month. That is how long they are told the trip is expected to take. The ship is stopping in Shanghai for a few days to pick up more passengers, and the sea is still full of live mines. Travel will be slow.

At dusk that evening, they wave goodbye to Japan. The girls have found a comfortable spot on top of a bunch of yellow ropes under a suspended lifeboat. There they sit and look out over the water towards the receding coastline of Japan.

-Will we ever come back?- Hannele wonders aloud.

-I will !- Baerbel says, while she is trying to climb the iron bars that hold the life-boat in place. -I'll bring my husband and children and show them our little house in Hakone and my tree house.-

-It will be much too far away from Germany,- Hannele says, shaking her head. -I think we'll never come back.-

-Let's sing,- Resel suggests and starts in her clear soprano voice. And soon 'Hoch Auf Dem Gelben Wagen' floats across the water. Three voices in harmony singing the song of the traveler on the stagecoach of life that stops only for so long at each phase of life and then travels on towards the inevitable end. Liesel has taught them this song, their Papa's favorite, and the girls feel sad for reasons they do not understand. Germany is an unknown entity for them, but Japan has been home for as long as they can remember. It holds all their memories. It is something with which they can identify.

In the East China Sea, the ship encounters the tail end of a major typhoon, and everyone is very sick. The dormitory begins to smell rather rancid, and Liesel and the girls spend as much time as possible on deck. But, in severe weather, that can be a rather dangerous business. A troop-transport does not have nearly as many safety railings as a passenger liner, and Liesel is always afraid that the children could get too close to the side and fall through the slack ropes that are tied along the outer edges of the decks.

Near Shanghai the water is muddy and yellow. More Germans board the ship. It takes them a week. Rumor has it that one resident German, who had lived there all his life, had wanted to stay and had hidden in the house of a Chinese friend. But it had been decided that all Germans were to be returned to Germany, and when he is eventually found, he is given no choice and brought on board.

The girls spend much time watching the activities on the quay. A row of prisoners in yellow and black striped overalls and chained one to the other, is marched in a large circle on the dusty pavement. The wind blows paper and sand along the dock, and the air is thick with the smell of refuse from the hundreds of houseboats crowded one against the other in the harbor.

As soon as the ship leaves Shanghai, one of the large mess halls is converted into an inoculation clinic. There had not been time to vaccinate the women and children before leaving Japan, and now a lot of catching up has to be done. Liesel is amazed at the many illnesses against which inoculation is now possible.

After the first three needles, the girls' arms start swelling up, red and hot, and sleeping becomes almost impossible, but at least they are spared the long waiting lines. They have never been afraid of doctors, and on the first day, they quietly wait their turn and then simply walk up and bravely hold out their arms. This causes quite a bit of comment in the over-crowded room where half the mothers are struggling to keep their children from running away. The next day, they do not have to wait at all.

-Where are those twins and their big sister?- one of the doctors calls out. -Let's have them up front here!- He takes Hannele's arm and holds it up. -Look, these young ladies are going to show you that it's nothing to be afraid of. See... nothing to it! - He tousles Hannele's hair and slips her a chocolate bar. - Thanks, that's a good girl.- Resel and Baerbel follow next.

While passing through the Red Sea, Liesel notices that Baerbel is unusually quiet and spends much of her time at the stern watching the foamy trail the ship leaves behind as it plows through the water. She remembers with a smile that Baerbel, when told that they would be passing through the Red Sea, had asked excitedly whether they were likely to see helmets and armor floating in the water. When no one could understand why she would think that, she patiently explained that, since so many of the Egyptian soldiers had been drowned while they were chasing Moses and the Israelites, maybe the odd sword or shield might still be seen floating around. Evidently she had not been convinced that this was highly unlikely.

It is now so unbearably hot in the below-deck sleeping quarters, that Liesel brings blankets and pillows up on deck, and she and the girls spend the nights under the stars. Early in the morning, however, the deck hands start scrubbing the steel floors, and everyone has to make a dash to the ovens below.

The ship passes through the Suez Canal at dawn, and Liesel wakes the girls to watch the sun rise over the desert. A caravan keeps pace with the ship for a short while, and then the camels lie down, and the riders dismount, and, kneeling on their colorful rugs, they bow towards Mecca.

-They are saying their morning prayers,- Liesel explains and hopes the girls will remember this scene. It is not something they are likely ever to see again.

At Port Said merchants come to the ship in little boats, and suddenly all the American soldiers are wearing red fezzes. Baerbel wants one too, but they are quite expensive, and she doesn't ask for one. Instead, she spends a lot of time talking sign language with the American M.P.s across the no-trespassing barriers that seem to be everywhere. She is hoping that her American friends might grow tired of their red hats and give her one.

The ship passes through the English Channel early in the morning, and later that day, the coast of Germany comes into view. Everyone is on deck, but it is very quiet. Liesel's throat hurts, so that she can hardly speak.

-Why are you crying, Mami?- Resel whispers. The girls are watching her, and it is true, the coast is a hazy outline through misty eyes, and she did not even know that she was crying.

-... Sixteen years.... I was a young woman then, running away to find a new life, to see the world. I never dreamt that I would see so much of it. To live so much! It seems like yesterday, and yet a century ago! A moment of blissful happiness and years of patient waiting, longing, hoping, wondering.... Gray hair, some aches and pains. Three bright-eyed buttercups opening to the sun, optimists all of them. What will the future hold?...-

-Tonight we will be on the Weser River,- she tells the girls with a smile. -A few more days, just a few more days, and we'll be home. -

XXI

Home again!
to see once more
the tranquil beauty
of your rolling hills
to hear the meadow lark
at break of day
and rest in quiet cottage
when the day is done
to feel your peace
pervade my weary mind
and breathe the air
that once caressed the brows
of men of thoughtfulness

So many years have gone
since last I walked
your rugged country trails
I thought of you at first
as something in my past
new places to explore
new friends to make
a life to live and love
on foreign shores
I was content

But now, a toy of life
battered and bruised
I yearn for calming breezes
friendly smiles
a babbling brook
the primrose on the hill
to find my roots again
and maybe thus

find rest.

*****

There is no one to greet the ship in Bremen, only an empty quay, windswept and dusty. Gray October clouds hang low over the harbor, and the cranes clang monotonously as they rummage in the black hole of the ship for trunks and luggage. It has taken six weeks to make the trip from Yokohama to Bremen, all of September and half of October.

-Where is Papa?- the girls want to know. -Maybe he did not know we were arriving this week?-

-No one is allowed near the docks,- Liesel tells them. Travelling in Germany is almost impossible now. One needs passports, signatures, and heaven knows what else. -Papa will be in Freiburg at the station, I am sure,- she tells the girls. But oh, how nice it would have been to see him here!

Once the luggage has been unloaded, everyone is finally allowed to disembark straight onto a waiting train. The children wave goodbye to their American army friends, who stand along the station platform, lazily chomping away at the ever-present chewing gum, and throw packages of it into the train windows.

Everyone is being taken to an old German detention camp, where all passengers are quartered for a few nights until the luggage can be sorted out and arrangements for transportation and passports to the various destinations in Germany's four occupied zones can be finalized.

In a closed-off section, behind barbed wire, German prisoners of war have now replaced the former occupants of the camp, whoever they may have been. Liesel doesn't want to think about it. The children stand for hours against the high wire fence and talk to the prisoners who want to know where they have come from and what they are doing here. However, most of the day is spent looking for suitcases among the huge pile which has been thrown at random right near the entrance gate.

Three times a day, food is ladled out onto tin plates from a field kitchen on the grounds. It is usually thin, watery soup with a few crackers. Liesel is beginning to feel like a prisoner of war herself, when, one evening, she sees a family of five, from the nearby town, searching through the garbage heaps at the back of the camp. She realizes then with a start, that all things considered, she and the girls have indeed been lucky.

At last, one evening, the train for French-occupied southern Germany is ready to leave. Kaete is going to her parents in Koeln, a city occupied by the English forces, and so the time has come to say good bye. She has been Liesel's best friend in all these years. Someone to count on, no matter what, who, though she would tease and scold sometimes, always understood. They will miss each other.

-Give my love to Willi,- she says, and Liesel sees her wiping her eyes for the first time since her Bernt was lost at sea. -I have your address. We'll keep in touch,- she promises. -Lord! I shall miss you and the girls!-

*****

The train rattles endlessly through the gray morning. Gusts of wind shake the windows and seep through the cracks of the ancient compartment, which, under normal conditions, would have been relegated long ago to the train graveyard. Liesel has made a bed for the twins by wedging her old blue travel trunk between two wooden benches. Hannele is sleeping on one of the benches, her head resting on Liesel's lap. It has been a long night.

Germany is passing by in the morning mist; low farmhouses with ancient thatched roofs, red-steepled churches, green meadows with fat cows. So peaceful, this countryside, but the cities tell a different story. There, charred ruins are witnesses of death and horror. Whole sections are gaping ruins, their occupants living in dark cellars, searching garbage dumps.

-Is most of Germany then like this?- Liesel wonders. -Most of Europe a rubble heap? Stark reminders of a world gone mad… .- She closes her eyes and thinks of Willi. -What will the years have done to him? What will he expect of me, and what will he see? I've grown older, and I have changed. There is no denying that. He used to think me beautiful…. The eyes of love!-

-'We will understand each other even better and become ever closer to one another, just as we did after our wedding day.' I know his letters by heart,- she thinks. -Then why am I afraid? That I have failed him somehow? That he will look for something in me and not find it? Years are deceivers of the mind, and memory is such a biased trickster. But no! This is just foolish nonsense! My ship is close to port and yet, I'm trembling, when for so long, I've longed for nothing but his arms.....-

-The children..... What will he think of our girls? And what will they think of him? I feel as though a rope around my heart is tightening. The anguish! Who would have thought this panic possible?-

-Will we be there today, Mami?-

-Will Papa be at the station to greet us?-

-Will he like us, Mami?-

-Are they worried too? Do they wonder what the next few days will hold in store for them? ... Yes, it has been a long night!-

***

In Frankfurt, everyone changes trains. The trunks and suitcases go aboard an ordinary passenger train, filled to capacity and more. -Now the last ties with Japan and the past are truly broken,- Liesel thinks. -We are no longer refugees in a foreign country, but ordinary German citizens, travelling on German soil.-

She soon realizes that she will have to teach the girls to speak more softly. They are used to not being understood on the crowded

Tokyo subway trains. Their accent too is high German, and all around them now, they hear the southern dialect.

To find a seat is clearly impossible. Some people are actually perched on the roofs of the cars. Baerbel accidentally steps on the toe of a large, perspiring lady in the crowded passageway.

-Watch what you are doing, child,- she screams and goes on in a frustrated tirade: -Why, we are nothing but cattle! That's how we are treated, cattle! I have lost all my belongings, everything! Everything, in the war! I've been on the road for two whole days already! But not a place to sit anywhere, not anywhere!-

People stare at her hysterics, and then Liesel hears Resel's voice, clear as a bell, -Only two days? Just imagine, *we*'ve been travelling since last August!- There is a sudden silence, as everyone turns to look at Resel. -Since August, eh? Where do you come from?- someone asks. But she is embarrassed, now that she realizes everyone has understood her, and she tries to pretend that she never said anything.

-We've come from Japan,- Liesel says quietly. -And, she's right, we *have* been underway since the end of August.-

Miraculously, three seats are vacated immediately, and Liesel and the girls are practically pushed into them, while what seems like half the people on the train crowd around to hear the details.

*****

259

The *Freiburger Muenster* can be seen long before the train pulls into the station. Its slender Gothic dome points toward a sunny, blue sky. -You'll always know Freiburg by its *Muenster,*- Willi had said many times. -There is no equal to it in all of Germany, for it was built with joy and grace by a lover's hand.-

-I'll help you unload those suitcases, Madam,- a young man volunteers, as the train comes to a stop in the partially bombed Central Station. The girls hold hands and cling to Liesel's coat. The pushing is unbelievable, and they don't want to get lost now. People are shouting and rushing towards the exit gate at the barrier that runs along the platform.

And then, Liesel stands alone on the platform, surrounded by three little girls and a pile of luggage. A man is staring at them from across the barrier. His face is very white, and his hands shake as he clenches the railing. His eyes speak of a thousand unshed tears.

Liesel's heart explodes within her breast, and the pounding in her ears grows louder. 'Willi!' Her lips shape the name, but no sound will come.

And he is over the barrier, and she is in his arms. -*Mein Liesele, mein Liesele*!- he sobs. And she is warm against him, and tears mingle with kisses.

How long, she does not know. Time has no meaning…. . Then, she looks up and sees three little faces watching from a distance. He sees them too, and his eyes light up as she used to remember them.

They are running towards him now, and he spreads his arms wide. And there is room for all of them.

****

Epilogue

I think of my family's five years in Germany as the happiest of my childhood. We were together, my mother and my father, a dear grandmother and an adopted uncle, Johann, who was more like the big brother I never had. We lived for a while in a little flat over a bakery. Two bedrooms, a kitchen and a toilet. On Saturdays, a big tin tub was brought into the kitchen and filled with very hot water, and we would bathe Japanese style: scrubbing and rinsing first, and then soaking, but not everyone at the same time. Mama and Papa shared the pull-out couch in the kitchen, which also housed *Oma* Fiand's knitting machine, with customers coming during the day, ordering knitted stockings, scarves, sweaters and even underwear. I learned how to sew these garments together with a special stitch and would often sit with *Oma* while she told me stories of growing up, one of ten children on a farm in Bavaria.

Later we moved to a hundred-year-old house, which had a small garden in the back by the kitchen window, where *Oma* grew pansies and geraniums, and we fed tiny red robins and yellow chickadees. There was a large yard in front where Papa built a chicken run and Baerbel and I learned how to ride a bicycle.

We also finally learned how to read, in a class with sixty other students, boys and girls, and *Fraulein* Zimmermann, who liked to use the strap. We carried little black slate boards to school because paper was scarce and scribblers were unheard of. And Baerbel got into punching fights with the kids who called us names because we did not speak German with a southern dialect, as they did.

Papa went to work on an old black bicycle, and when he got home late at night, we would all climb into bed with him, and he would read to us from the novels he had picked up at the English consulate, translating them on sight in order to keep up his English. We read *David Copperfield* and *Huckleberry Finn* and *White Fang,* and Mama would climb into bed with us and pretend she was a little girl too. On Sundays, we would hike in the Black Forest mountains, and Papa would tell us of Dehra Dun, where, towards the end of the war, the prisoners had been allowed to leave the camp on day parole, and he had done some mountain climbing and had lived many strange adventures. No one had ever escaped from the camp, except one man, Heinrich Harrer, an experienced mountain climber, and the men at Dehra Dun never found out that he had made it across the mountains into Tibet.

Baerbel and I went for recorder lessons to an elegant spinster lady who lived in a flat overlooking the Dreisam River and had a wonderful grand piano in her living room. And Hannele took violin lessons from a crusty old teacher who frightened her. Later, I also received a violin and Baerbel a cello, and we all set off to the university for music lessons. When visitors came to the house, Mama and Papa invariably asked us to perform, which we hated, and I am sure, the visitors did too.

But we spent many happy evenings singing with Papa and Mama and learning the lyrics of dozens of German folk-songs.

Then, one cold January day, Papa and Mama told us that we would soon be going on a long voyage again, to a big country in North America, called Canada. Papa would be leaving first to find a job and a place for us to live in a city called Montreal. He would join a friend there, who had been a prisoner of war in Canada and had loved the country, and who was now living in Montreal and would help us get settled there.

I don't remember being upset at this news. It was one more adventure, and we were used to travelling around. But our *Oma* decided not to come with us, and that was a hard thing to accept. That was the only thing that hurt.

For Papa, Germany had been a big disappointment. The roots he had tried to plant there had not taken. The war had destroyed what he remembered or what he had thought all along he remembered. And he too had changed. He did not fit in now, anymore than he did when he was a boy of sixteen. And so his new hope was Canada. He left in April on a ship sailing out of Hamburg and landed at the now famous Pier 21 in Halifax. We followed in October and left *Oma* at the garden gate, waving good bye to the five happy years she had spent with us.

Our first view of Canada was its autumn glory. Sailing up the Saint Lawrence River in October was an unforgettable experience! On both sides of the river miles of color, dotted here and there by small villages and silver-steepled churches. This would be our new home. It took our breath away.

This time, Papa was at the dock in Quebec City, and we waved to him from the deck of the *Canberra*. He looked small, so far below us, and a little frail. A night train had been arranged for all the immigrants going on to Montreal, and Papa had large red apples for us and Butterfinger chocolate bars.

Montreal was cold. We lived in a boarding house, sharing a kitchen with the landlady who had three cats. Hannele, Baerbel and I slept in a tiny room, just big enough for a double bed. I slept in the middle, and before falling asleep, we would play all sorts of games, usually of a competitive nature: who could hold her breath the longest; who could stare without blinking for the longest time; who could be the first to name a city, river and country starting with the letter 'F', and, on a less refined level, who could burp the loudest. But as I could not burp on command, I never won that one.

Upon his arrival in Montreal, Papa had almost immediately found employment with the Canadian National Railway. There was opportunity for advancement, and he was happy. We soon moved to a larger flat on the Lakeshore, and Papa brought home appliances and furnishings from his trips to places like Chicago, Vancouver and Halifax. We went to school by bus and learned to speak English and a bit of French. And during our first summer, we earned money by weeding large flowerbeds and mowing the grounds of a wealthy gentleman who lived by the lake.

And then, suddenly, Papa became very ill. An operation revealed advanced cancer with no hope of recovery. He died on Christmas Eve 1953, less than two years after first setting foot on Canadian soil. And so his dream and our childhood came to an end.

Hannele went to work as soon as she turned sixteen. The parish priest paid the rent, and the nuns, who taught us, supplied baskets of groceries. Johann came over from Germany and helped to support us, and Mama sewed. We survived.

***

Mama died on January 22, 1973, at the age of seventy-one in the advanced stages of Parkinsons disease. She is buried with Papa at the Catholic Cemetery in Dorval, Quebec.

***

I don't visit Montreal very often anymore. We have all three moved to other parts of the continent, and I have very few friends who still live in Quebec. And so, years will often pass between my visits to the little cemetery where Mama and Papa sleep in peace, finally together for eternity. On one such visit, on my way to give a poetry reading in northern Quebec, this poem was born, which I dedicate to their memory:

> So this is where they sleep
> one with the other
> for ever now
> the promise to be one

I Cry For Innocence

"Love is Eternal"
engraved in stone

The words have faded long ago
and yet
they echo in my mind
a melody
in perfect pitch
as sun slants golden
on this plot of land
and early buds of spring
bravely declare that
life goes on
though here they sleep...

A resting place
in ground which held for him
a foreign touch
cold Canada
that claimed his wandering soul and
left her to the lonely task
of twenty years of living

-I feel again warm breezes of
a tropic sky
I see the smiles of youth and health
and hear the carefree promise of
a future to be shared in love-

Buds only
whose bloom was scorched by war
and cruel parting

a life of momentary hopes
for better times to come

Cold Canada
held out the last such hopeful moment
a quiet plot of land
here by the silver steeple
and sleep - together now
beneath the budding trees
black granite
and the words
"Love is Eternal"

****

Hannele married and raised five children. She and her husband left Quebec upon retirement and now live in Peterborough, Ontario, near their two daughters.

Baerbel completed a doctorate in existential philosophy at DePaul University in Chicago. A Sister of Notre Dame de Namur, she publishes extensively and travels and lectures throughout the United States, Canada, and abroad.

Resel married and raised four children. She obtained a doctorate in Canadian Comparative Literature at the Université de Sherbrooke, Quebec, and teaches at the Université de Moncton. She lives with her husband in Riverview, New Brunswick.